Actual Mileage

Stories

by

Max Zimmer

from

Kit Car Builder Magazine

2006 — 2014

Actual Mileage

From Kit Car Builder Magazine

2006 — 2014

These forty-seven stories, in most cases, are about real people, and tell mostly real things about them. In some cases, the people and the stories dip into fiction, where they are either products of the author's imagination or used in a fictitious way. As a general rule, since there isn't any way of knowing when this happens, no reference to any real person or event should be taken as literal or factual without prior consent.

Max Zimmer
Copyright ©2014 by Max Zimmer

Front cover illustration by Cory Drake
Back cover author photo by Cory Drake

Cover design by Phoenix Design

All forty-seven stories in this book were originally published in *Kit Car Builder* magazine as columns under the heading "Actual Mileage." They are included as they originally appeared, with the permission of Jim and Carolyn Youngs, editor and publisher of *Kit Car Builder*.

ISBN 978-0-9854481-8-9

No animals or cars were harmed in the creation of these stories.

For Jim and Carolyn Youngs

Also by the author:

Journey

and

Of the World

Books 1 and 2 of the trilogy

If Where You're Going Isn't Home

Contents

Introduction

In "Getting Ants Drunk," a couple spend a humid summer afternoon on their deck serving drops of Malibu Rum to ants that fall from overhead trees onto their table.

In "Under the Floor," a trap door in the concrete floor of a garage takes a man back forty years to his first rustbucket Porsche Speedster and the still incomprehensible breakup of his young first marriage, and then returns him to the present having learned how to love what he's lucky enough to have had a second chance at.

At a VFW club in "Amazing Grace," a bellydancer does an astonishing dance with a sword balanced on her head. Afterward, she comes to the bar where you buy her a drink, learn that she's a pipefitter by day, and hear her spellbinding story about working on a Hoboken rooftop the morning the planes came down the Hudson just over her head and plunged through the towers.

In "No Requiem," members of a car club meet one last time to celebrate its life, honor its death, share stories, and toast their surviving friendship.

In "Jimmy," a New York street guy sails the sidewalks of the East Thirties in a mangy overcoat, unlaced workboots, dreadlocks, an indestructible smile, and a passionate determination to repay a two dollar loan.

In "Veterans Day," an uncle takes the orphaned son he inherited from a Vietnam veteran to the back woods of Pennsylvania for an afternoon of car building with a couple of his buddies.

In "Distance Traveled," two Jersey guys sip mojitos in their chaises on a Dominican Republic beach and compare notes on how far they've ever driven for a girl they loved.

And in "Ghost Riders," a Maryland couple search the Atlantic Seaboard for other folks with Speedster replicas to go cruising with, a quest that starts as a dream and ends up coming real in a phenomenal gathering from all across North America.

These are just a few samplings of the forty-seven stories gathered in this collection. All of them first appeared in the magazine *Kit Car Builder* under the heading "Actual Mileage."

When I was hired in 2006 to write a human interest column for the magazine, my new boss gave me two rules. One was to keep each story to a page. The other was to write about anything I wanted as long as I put a car in the mix somewhere. Not just any car. A hand-built car. A reproduction of one or another car that stands as an icon in our collective automotive dreamscape. A postwar MG. A 50s Porsche Speedster. An array of historic racecars, jazz age classics, hot rods, original designs, and in particular the Ford Cobra of the 60s. After all, it was a magazine about special cars, and putting a special car in the mix kept what I wrote legitimate.

More than cars, however, these stories are about equally special people. Most of them are real — as real as their autographs on the cover of this book — although what I sometimes do with them is fiction and slips in some cases into fantasy. But they're people drawn together, the way people everywhere are, by a shared passion, a collective lunacy, the urge to make a dream they have in common real. You'll recognize them. You'll get to know them by name as they come and go over the eight year stretch these stories run. For the most part they move in relative anonymity through the real world. They have jobs, mothers, facebook pages, grandkids, pets, spouses, sailboats, favorite beers, places to live. They just happen to have a set of keys and a roadway to a parallel world — one where they build the cars they dream about and love and then take them out and drive them. From rides through the rolling wooded hills of New England to cruises down the coast highway to cross country road trips. Hot Springs to Knotts Berry Farm. Ottawa to Key West. Vermont to Pennsylvania. California to Kansas. You'll recognize their stories too, because they're stories of the human experience we all share, with a car put in the mix somewhere, but then cars are in the mix of our lives anyway.

You'll also run across names of the manufacturers and suppliers whose goods and services make this dream world real. You'll meet Steve Temple and Harold Pace, writers for hire like me, and Jim and Carolyn Youngs, editor and publisher of the magazine that gave these stories a home and made this collection possible.

Finally, you'll read about a special place in Pennsylvania called Carlisle, a four-day annual national gathering place for what we call the Madness, a field of automotive dreams where magical and marvelous and momentous things can happen if you can only imagine them.

2006

Pimped Rides, Shared Illusions

"You ever feel bad about doing this?"

"Doing what?"

"Using your car to get free stuff."

Rocky and me are sitting under the shade of a tree at the edge of this meadow in Waterloo Village. About sixty feet out our Speedsters sit side by side in the grass with a mix of maybe twelve other cars. The place has some of the sixties rock concert provenance of places like Woodstock and the bog at Watkins Glen, but these days it's used for wine and beer and poetry festivals and musical retrospectives. We're here because of Rich. Rich is a member of The Wanderers and the guy in charge of picking cars for these events. He's got his 55 Bel Air here, along with a couple of old black flivvers, a Mustang GT 500, a hideaway hardtop Ford, and a fifty-something Packard once owned by Samantha from *Bewitched*. The event is a combo wine festival and Beatles retrospective. To our left, under a huge open-sided tent with a stage, bands have been playing Beatles tunes since noon. Toni and Linda are over there dancing barefoot in the grass. People are walking around with wineglasses, wearing hospital bracelets to prove that they paid to be here, looking our cars over. We're here for free. Free admission, free drinks, free food. Alan Parsons is singing. Todd Rundgren, whose tune "Hello It's Me" is on Toni's short list of hits, is due to take the stage soon. Some guy is bent over behind Rocky's Speedster with his head down underneath the engine lid. Another guy, on his knees, is pondering my left front wheel.

"Why should I feel bad?" Rocky says.

"You know. Like a pimp or something."

"A pimp. Hmmm."

"Yeah. There's my car out there doing all the work. Here's me getting all the perks."

Out in the meadow a skinny young kid with a head of tousled thick black hair circles my car taking pictures with a monster digital camera.

"Maybe I should get it an apartment," I say.

"Your car?"

"Yeah. It's what pimps do."

"Get apartments for their cars?"

"Some nice french furniture. A fireplace. Red velvet curtains."

"You scare me."

"Vanity plates."

Rocky likes hot dogs. It doesn't take much to remind him. This is one of those times. He gets up.

"You want anything?" he says.

"Thanks. I'm fine."

"Sure you are."

I was in the eighth grade the first time I saw a Porsche. Pedaling home from school when it came up behind me and went on ahead. I had no idea what it was. But it became the only car I ever wanted. I remember trying to chase it down to get another look. Searching through the parking lot of a Safeway's on the way. Feeling stupid for thinking that someone with a car that magical would ever need to shop for milk or toothpaste. For years I sustained the illusion that I could live without milk and toothpaste too if I had a car like that. I imagined European roads that never ended and drove them. Later on, I was lucky enough to own one, then luckier still to learn that I could recreate the one I'd owned. At events like this I don't like hanging around it because of the questions that inevitably lead to the "original versus replica" dialogue. I've never found a way that is simultaneously simple and honest to answer them. What year it is. What kind of engine it has. If I restored it myself. If the flares are stock. The simple answers are lies. The honest answers are technical and complicated. They also tend to defeat the magic. Not because it's a replica. But because that's what technical and complicated answers do. Take away the ability to imagine. Dispel the illusion. And so I park it, walk away, sit where I can take protective action if I need to, and let people take what they want from the experience. Pimp it. Sometimes, when people ask and Rocky's handy, I tell them it's his car.

I spend the next few hours talking to Rich and some of the other Wanderers. Get myself a hot dog. Bask in the shade sipping Jersey wines. Hear the opening notes of "Hello It's Me" and realize I'll have to peel Toni off the undercarriage of Rundgren's bus before I can call the afternoon over. Periodically, I see the skinny kid with the tousled hair appear again, take another round of pictures, then stand there. The last few times he's there he leaves the camera hanging at his side. Just stands there looking. The Wanderers eventually leave.

Then Rocky. I figure I'll get things ready before I go looking for Rundgren's bus. As I reach the car a family of adults strolls up. One of the women approaches me and asks if it's my car. She's got an accent that sounds Russian or Greek. She has some trouble walking like she's recovering from surgery or maybe lightly crippled. I look around for Rocky. He's gone.

"Yes," I say.

She smiles. "It is just beautiful," she says.

No questions. Just an openly frank observation in a voice that turns my bones to butter. She asks if she can have her picture taken next to it. I look her over for sharp protruding objects. I know I'm about to break the cardinal rule of showing a car. The rule about not touching one unless you're naked. But everything I see looks soft, and I can't help myself.

"How about inside it?" I suggest.

She looks astonished. "Really?"

I open the door, help her in, stand back while the rest of her family gathers along the sides. Someone raises a camera. All of them thank me. Nobody asks me anything about the car. Just privately take it for what it means to them. Accepting their gratitude for something that didn't cost me anything, I remember the skinny kid with the camera, and start wishing I'd given him the same opportunity.

And then he's there. Out of breath. Shy but animated.

"Can I?" he says.

I open the door. He hands me his camera.

"Can you take a picture of me?"

I step out in front of the car but can't figure out the camera. One of the men from the family suddenly comes back, takes it out of my hands, snaps a couple of pictures of the kid. Through the windshield I can see his hands on the wheel and the way his grin infuses his entire face. I have to go way back — maybe to my own first Porsche — to remember feeling joy that pure and unconditional on my own face. People are leaving the Village along the fenced path behind the car. "He'll remember that the rest of his life!" someone shouts. Yeah, I stand there thinking, I know. There are people who call our cars — to put it politely — illusions. Maybe so. But illusions aren't about what they are. They're about what they do. And what they do is too original and real and lasting not to share.

Engines

Cliff Scott was president of the New Jersey Replicar Club from 2001 through 2003. For seven years before that, he was secretary and editor of the Replicar Roundup, the monthly newsletter. Three years before that, when Tim Lewis founded the club, Cliff was a founding member. Tim still has the Grand Sport he used to race around Louden. But he's moved on to the IHRA as owner of Doug Foley's Torco Race Fuels top fuel dragster. Cliff's moved on too. Two weeks ago, after fighting a running guerilla war with cancer that started before I met him eight years ago, he passed away.

When Cliff became president, I took over as secretary and editor, tasked with recording our meetings and events and putting the Roundup together. The mailing list included around 90 members and a host of other clubs around the country. Cliff was my mentor. I asked him if the club had an editorial policy. "I'll give you the one I used," he responded. "Why say it in five words when you can use fifty." It was like giving a car thief the key to the City of Detroit. I took his four-page template and blew it out to sixteen pages. Last week, looking to put together a retrospective for his wife Bobbi, I reviewed the Roundups I'd written under his stewardship.

I'd forgotten how far I'd run with Cliff's editorial counsel. How I'd fabricated one running fantasy after another and folded them in with the true stuff to make them believable by association. How I'd left these fabrications out there, gathering the patina of truth, not only among the members of the club who didn't attend meetings, but also among people like Vern Hance, Ben Miller, Ken and Meha Smith, Cliff Speck, Bill Kinsey, Randy Sheltgen, and Don Shank, people I swapped newsletters with, earnest and dedicated people who must have wondered what exotic metals had seeped into the Jersey aquifer. It's time to set the record straight.

No. Cliff never brought twenty years of Playboy Playmates to a meeting. Kim Basinger, the Women of Washington, the Nebraska State cheerleaders, all lies. The skinny Belgian girl from Sex in Cinema never sat on my knee. We never held a meeting in a Boeing 747 while Bill, a retired Continental pilot, circled Newark. We never did a Christmas show-and-tell where guys brought things like a black-footed ferret in a Hush Puppies shoebox, a Rival crockpot cooker, a purple Lava Psychedelic Swirl Motion Lamp, roller blades. Old George never did the Howdy Doody thing with the Chia Head Professor on his knee. Paul never bit guys in the butt with a Martha Stewart Fruit Harvester. And Martha Stewart never came to a meeting. Neither did Johnny Rutherford, Marcus Welby, Tom Petty and the Heartbreakers, Nick Carraway, Simply Red, or Norman Vincent Peale. Bill never ran the Strategic Air Command or flew Air Force One for Reagan, Cliff never owned Newark, Tommy never taught the Pope Mandarin, Mark was never secretly married to Beverly Sills, Phil wasn't the inventor of all the $19.99 stuff on TV, and Warren wasn't the missing Beatle. Finally, Cliff never had a single drink at a single meeting. The silver flask of Four Roses he always brought and shared with me to where faces started melting around the room? Another lie.

I guess I'd wanted this stuff to be true. Last week, reading through it, I even found myself believing it. "Wow," I told Toni. "Cliff ran some awesome meetings." I felt her hand on my shoulder. "Honey," she said, in her cautious way of reminding me there's a nursing home in my future, "you made most of that stuff up. Remember?"

Here's what was true about Cliff. He came to most every meeting in the same outfit, nondescript work pants, suspenders, an old STP or Isky teeshirt, glasses, and a gavel, ready to do business in the break room of Warren's warehouse. He wasn't tall, but he was formidable, a solid guy with a big face, crewcut white hair that started high back on his forehead, a white moustache, the cup of a white beard around his chin. He had the wry and tough and open humor of a Jersey guy, the gentle and unsentimental disposition of an engineer, the big impartial heart you'd want in both a father and a boss. He drove a white MGTD he built on a bug he pilfered from his daughter. He papered the entire ceiling of his garage with Playboy centerfolds to have something to contemplate from his creeper. When I first joined, the Sistine Chapel was a little church in Italy. Since then, in the parlance of the club, it has come to mean Cliff's garage.

We're a band of unrelated characters without a socially defensible reason to ever occupy the same room. Any two of us together is an oxymoron. Our cars are the same way. Auburn, Healey, Cobra, Speedster, Gazelle, Allard, Baron, Bugatti, Daytona, Super Seven,

Diva, Frasier Nash, MGTD, GTB, Boxer, Dennan, GT40, 500K, SS-100, Humvee. Cliff celebrated this diversity. Gave us a playground as big as Kansas. Understood too how inadvertent and volatile our convergence was. The unifying force it needed. He became that force. Every meeting followed a rolling and strictly held agenda. Every event was scheduled, delegated, cobbled together, attended. He relentlessly advocated participation. Whenever we came un-glued, we got the crack of his gavel and his trademark baritone call to order: "One meeting!" He continues to be the force at the heart of what holds our club together, its eclectic legacy, its collective prove-nance.

He's not alone. There are the people I mentioned earlier, people I apologize for not yet knowing, people who for years have put their time and work and talent into building and sustaining the local, re-gional, and virtual clubs that are the engine rooms of this commu-nity, people who have always been its strong and tireless and indis-pensable engines. Cliff was one of you.

Walks in Water

The Saturday in September 2004 when Hurricane Ivan crawls into the Northeast. In a house in the hills of Pennsylvania, across the Delaware from Jersey, I'm standing in the kitchen, eating the best quesadilla I've ever tasted. Four hours ago, on my ride up, I hit detours everywhere, drove through mud, branches, spontaneous rivers, got lost so long I started looking for Welcome to Oklahoma signs. The way roads were being closed I'm still surprised I got here. Just outside, a pump is pulling knee-deep water out through a basement window, and across the yard, in a pole barn so obscured by rain you have to trust your memory, my Speedster's got a new engine tucked up its rear, hooked up, ready to fire. The awesome part about the quesadilla is that a 33-year-old automotive wizard in greasy levis and a dusty black teeshirt just whipped it up for me. Wade. Indian, he said once, for Walks in Water.

"Where'd you learn to cook like this?"

"I used to be a chef," he says.

"You're kidding. Where?"

"Different places. Krogh's, the Thirsty Moose, the Publick House."

"The Publick House? When?"

"From 90 to 94 maybe."

"How about 92? August 8th?"

"What day?"

"Saturday."

"Yeah. I worked every Saturday. Why?"

The big brick inn that dates back to the Revolution. Me and the mayor of Chester waiting under the big tree out in back. An entourage of women coming out, petals of a flower, my bride at their breathtaking center. The mayor telling me she's better looking than I am. Me betting him he says that to all the grooms. Him saying no, actually, he's seen some pretty ugly brides. The reception afterward in the big colonial room inside, tablecloths, a jazz trio, a private menu. On a top ten list of things you never expect to be telling your mechanic may be things like, "Wow. I've had the same toes for 62 years." But the one I'm about to spring on Wade has got to be Number One.

"You cooked for my wedding."

He eases his quesadilla back out of his mouth. "No," he says.

"Yeah. You did."

Wade's 12 when he starts doing cars. Oil changes, tuneups, brakes for the old family Chrysler Cordoba. He's 15 when he hotwires an 84 Buick Celebrity, the only new car his folks will ever have, and slams it into a tree at 85, hard enough to squirt the engine out through the grill. He gets a year's suspension effective the minute he gets his license. At 16, he starts washing dishes at Krogh's, because it's the closest job he can hitchhike to. Soon he's doing menus, moving up as cook, then as sous chef, at places like Shenani-gan's, the Thirsty Moose, Basking Ridge Country Club, the Publick House.

He spends 11 years cooking for strangers. Gets good at it. Among other awards he takes first place at the Perona Farms Food Show for his "Shrimp Sabol." But cooking isn't it. Something borne of an accident. A place to ride out the wild seed sown by a lunatic family. He'll tell you about getting a spatula hot enough in fryer grease to where it can melt synthetic fabric, then slipping it into the dishwasher's back pocket. About fires. Food fights. About the Mother's Day he hurls an egg from outside the back door in through the kitchen at another cook. The guy ducks. The egg keeps going, out through the serving window, straight across the dining room, where a thirtyish woman heading for the restroom walks her silk blouse right into its path. She goes down screaming. Takes what she's dripping with for blood. "I've been shot! I've been shot!" No. He doesn't get fired. He's gotten to be too good at what he does.

Cars are always there. Votech courses. Apprenticeships at dealer shops. He equips his first car, a 72 Chevelle, with the engine out of a junked Jimmy dualie. Fixes cook and waitress cars in parking lots. One afternoon, looking at a 79 Firebird, he decides to clean the engine. Take off the air cleaner, manifold, valve covers, water pump, other parts, run them through the kitchen dishwasher. There, in the confluence of kitchen grease and engine grease, his worlds come close enough to touch, long enough to let him cross from the accidental one back to the real one. He gets a job at my local garage. This tough young silent crewcut guy with the most instinctual automotive touch I've seen. Within a year, he's talking his own business, and after he single-handedly builds the pole barn out across the yard, he does it. Names it Kartooning out of this childhood admiration for Mickey Mouse. In his kitchen we're still on my wedding.

"So? How'd you like the food?" he asks.

"It sucked."

"Really?"

"Everything sucks in a tux. Nothing personal."

"Okay. Long as it was the tux."

He'll tell you this stuff when you ask, when you're waiting for headers to cool, hurtling along a decomposing backwoods road in his rat Mustang at a hundred twenty, and one of the possible ways the upcoming curve will take you is the afterlife. You'll wonder why you let this guy anywhere less than the length of Argentina near your car. But by then he's got you. You've seen his other side. Not the side where he hands you an M-16 and points to a shredded barrel on the hill across his pond. Not the side where he raises game hens for food and then falls for them too hard to even eat their eggs. But the transcendent automotive genius side. Bring him a car and watch him turn into the most intensely serious and focused guy you know. We'll get to that. To local garages lining up their cars and calling him over for diagnostic walkdowns. To Car Talk keeping him on call as a technical expert. To the retired satellite engineer who works around the shop and gives me trumpet lessons. To the kid too scared to drive his Lightning once he gets it back. Wade's World. We just got here.

Death by Association

A friend in Idaho recently had his neighborhood call to tell him they'd gotten complaints about him parking two vehicles in his driveway overnight. There's a "covenant" that limits him to one. That vehicle has to be a daily driver. He wanted to know who'd complained. No good. There's another "covenant" that shields these snitches — he calls them "Parking Nazis" — with anonymity when they report an "infraction." My friend's a car guy. Five last I counted. I hadn't known that he lived in one of those — half kidding here — lockstep zombie neighborhoods governed by a "homeowners' association."

First, where I'm from, a covenant is something you make with God or Lucifer, not with strangers who want to tell you what to do with your property without offering to weed your flowerbeds. Second, I wonder on whose planet, orbiting around a dark star inside whose skull, it became an "infraction" to use your driveway for the reason driveways were invented. Third, to my list of reasons to shoot myself, I can add this question if I'm ever heard to ask it: "Then what, sir, would you like me to use my driveway for?"

Take a neighborhood, border it with Belgian blocks, and sell the houses to people looking for covenants to live by. Whose idea was this? Who found this lost Twilight Zone episode? I don't know. I've got several friends who've ended up in these places around the country. They're clueless too. All my friend in Houston knows is that he can only paint his house three pre-approved shades of beige. All my friend in Hartford knows is that he has to get approval for anything he wants to plant. All my friend in Scottsdale knows is that he can't drink a beer on his porch unless it's from a colored bottle. All my friend outside Columbus knows is that he has to park his painter's van in a lot out by the gate and then walk home from there in his clown-bespattered coveralls. And my friend in Idaho — all he knows is that every night he's gotta stash four cars in a two-car garage.

I hesitate going after these organizations because, when you make them human and view them from the rear, they're too exposed and graceless in their plumed and militant foolishness to make a fair target. But I can't help speculating on their mindset. Maybe something like this. We don't need to know anything about your life. We don't need to know that you like orange shingles or five-story birdhouse mailboxes or lawn statues of Tolkien elves, or that you cultivate begonias or collect miniature windmills or barbecue jackrabbits, or that you drink Olympia, or listen to reggae while you pop dandelion roots, or build cars. In fact, the closer to dead you can play, the better we'll like it.

I live in an association too, an older one, a "lake community." It was founded in 1926, by Germans, many of whom my Idaho friend wasn't all that surprised to hear were real Nazis, who built a dam across a small valley and then needed money to maintain the artificial lake they were stuck with. We've got rules too. Luckily, eighty years have worn the place down, left it with some wisdom and forbearance, because nobody reports the two-foot weeds out front around my lamppost, the moldering Interstate battery I keep circling with the mower, or the vehicles — a busted BMW, a ratty 911, a seized Trans Am — I've let my sons and neighbors sideline on my extra parking area out by the street. It's still a far cry — and 800 dollars in dues — from the neighborhoods I grew up in.

They were neighborhoods where, if you were lunatic enough to want to turn your front yard into a pineapple orchard, that's what you went ahead and did. My favorite was a small street lined with two-story houses, small, sturdy, sided with asphalt brick. Half the yards were packed dirt. Rickety barbecue grills stood off the front porches. Second-floor bedroom windows were opened for morning air. Tired old boats of cars were parked everywhere. A Buick Electra with its bleached hood in the air, an Olds 88 with its big rear end on jackstands, a Grand Marquis with half the naugahyde scraped off its Landau roof. Rules were improvised and then discarded. If you ticked off your neighbor he'd find a sociable way to tell you. The street had the comfy and easy feel and vaguely roguish attitude of a favorite uncle home on leave. You could smell it. Armpit sweat, beer, gas, oil, grease, exhaust, fish, cabbage, ham hocks and beans, every supper cooking in every house you passed on your way home to your own supper. You could hear it. Your mother making the street ring with your name. Kids practicing violin and piano and concertina. The chime of a dropped wrench falling through an engine compartment to the dirt. Parents fighting unashamedly, because discord is, after all, the harmonic counterpart to bliss. You could see and feel it. Families on a street. Real, raw, open, groping our way together through the human adventure. The one abiding rule? You didn't tattle.

When did neighborhoods lose this? When did they adopt the forced and absurd shoulder-to-shoulder remoteness of a passenger jet? When did they become these beige graveyards of tended mausoleums whose driveways have to be vacated in case the night children come out to play hopscotch? These Orwellian associations where a covenant of anonymity turns neighbors into stoolies? You want to tell me what I can park in my driveway? Fine. Buy my house, be my landlord, and I'll pay you a dollar a year in rent.

Back in the 70s my dad bought one of those Arizona desert lots they promised to build a town around and never did. If I had Bill Gates' money, of course I'd try to eradicate AIDS, and buy every kindergarten kid in the world a laptop, but I'd keep enough to do what my dad did and see it through. Buy a piece of land the size of a cattle ranch. Cut it into lots big enough to give car haulers room to turn around. Build modest houses out front. Hire a thousand Amish guys to build 20-car pole barns out back. Make up my own rules. Starting with driveways.

2007

The Soul of an Old Machine

Last night, three generations of family took their chairs around the big oak poker table in our dining room. Before we dug in to an unpardoned turkey, a spiral cut ham, pot roast, and a host of steaming side dishes, each of us acknowledged something we were thankful for. A promotion to head welder. A good report card. A fat raise. Soldiers. Mommy was a popular one. Not wanting to hurt anyone's feelings and hand them an easy excuse to leave before they did the dishes, when it came my turn, I said, "Every one of you." I expected groans. I got them. But I meant it. The people who make up this family — including those who couldn't be here yesterday — are light years out in front of anything else I could be blessed with.

But this is an automotive magazine, and not the *Reader's Digest*, behooving me to be thankful for things in my life with engines. First, of course, for my Speedster. Second, for my Audi S4, tricked out to horsepower and torque ratings of 360 and 380. Third, for Toni's S2000, and the chance to ride shotgun next to her, there for anyone who knows the difference to see that the woman I'm married to can drive a stick.

But wait. There's more. A fourth car, one that has no obvious place in an automotive magazine, with the dubious exception of Car Shopper.

Toni and I are writers for hire for power plants. We live in the northwest corner of Jersey, in the rolling rural foothills that lead west into the Poconos and north into the Catskills. East of us, and then southeast, is the corridor that gives the state its reputation, the industrial and urban landscapes that lie this side of the Hudson River and the harbor from New York. You can see them through Tony Soprano's windows when he's driving up the Turnpike at the opening of the show. The skyline of Newark huddled against the long backdrop of Manhattan. The arc of the Bayonne Bridge. The long lazy rolling black trusswork of the Pulaski Skyway. Jets escaping the yellow air of Newark Airport. The cranes and container yards of Port Elizabeth. Smokestacks. All kinds of smokestacks, rising from the banks of burned-out rivers like the Hackensack and the Passaic, out toward Newark Bay, south toward the Arthur Kill, the open throat of water that separates Jersey from Staten Island. Most of the stacks that are still in service belong to power plants, plants you reach along thin dissolving causeways across the marshlands, through the exhausted neighborhoods of homely towns, past truck and railroad yards, impound lots for the cars stolen out of Newark, Elizabeth, Union, Irvington, the hollow windows of old red brick factories abandoned too long ago to be sued for cleaning up the mercury they leached into the water table, places where lower Manhattan is close enough across the water that the hole in the sky where the towers were still catches you, still takes your breath, no matter how many times you've seen it. Beyond these Jersey landmarks, across the harbor and the river, the gotham of Manhattan and its gauntlet of tunnels, bridges, and brokeback highways to the other boroughs, the Bronx, Queens, Brooklyn, Kennedy Airport, Long Island, to other plants we write for.

Leaving a plant with piping diagrams, operating instructions, system walkdown notes in the back seat, driving back across the marshlands in this largely derelict industrial battlefield, you tend to get existential. But this is an automotive magazine, not the *International Journal of Applied Philosophy*, behooving me to get back to what this column is about. The fourth car. The car we happen to be riding in. The only car we'd ever trust out here. Not a steal-me-red S4, or a jack-me-yellow S2000, or a hock-me-silver Speedster, but a 1993 Mazda 626, thirteen years old, 150 grand on the odometer, dirty white paint, the interior some nameless beige, the fatigued but invincible iron soul of an old and anonymous soldier. For ten years now, it's the only car that takes us into the long sick congested industrial urban heart of the tri-state corridor. Newark. Grandma's house, across the South Bronx on the Cross-Bronx Expressway, where the overpasses are fitted with tall chainlink fences to keep kids from lobbing bricks and other street debris down into the paths of approaching cars. Plants in east Jersey, the New York boroughs, Long Island. And brings us home again. It's our rat. Newark rat, city rat, Grandma rat. Hudson, Sewaren, Kearny, Bergen, Linden, or 58th Street rat, depending on the plant we're visiting.

Its sister cars, of course, get the fluff rides. When we hit a plant in upstate New York, or out in Pennsylvania, it's the Audi that gets to stretch its legs on the interstates. When we go to Watkins Glen, it's the Honda that gets to rub shoulders with the 911s. When I get myself lost in the rolling hills west and north of here, it's in the

Speedster. The spoiling doesn't end there. The Speedster's got a Gene Berg five-speed on its wish list. A month ago the Audi got a set of EBC rotors and ceramic pads. Next are bigger intercoolers. The S2000 gets supercharged when the price drops into the range of sanity. The Mazda? The only thing it's ever had on its list is whatever wears out or breaks.

It knows it's old. Knows it's tired. Knows that its tappets clatter, its transmission isn't so quick to downshift, its headlights have lost their luster. Knows that it has to sit outside in winter in the steady blast of frigid wind here on the ridge, in spring and fall when its paint gets nubbed with sap and stained with pollen and its cracks get clogged and silted with seeds and leaves off the trees, in summer when mice nest in the blower cage of its heater and spiders build webs up in its undercarriage. Knows there's no room for it among the prima donnas in the garage. Knows its suspension parts are cheap enough not to bankrupt us if it breaks a strut on some urban chuckhole deep enough to see the subway through. Knows that its value to us is that it's too nondescript, too old, too ugly for anyone to want to steal.

We don't name cars. We just call it the Mazda. But an obvious choice would be Cinderella. The trouble is that we'd be raising its expectations. Making it think there might be a fairy godmother, glass slippers, a fancy ball, the automotive counterpart of a handsome prince in its future. There simply isn't. What lies ahead for it is this. We'll drive it long enough to get our son through college. Then we'll replace it, hand it down to one of the kids as the sacrificial first car, the car that gets totaled in the rite-of-passage accident every kid has to have. It won't take much to total it. Our genius mechanic Wade will bring it back, its nose wrinkled, shards of plastic where the grill was, its headlights held in place with juryrigged shelf brackets, uglier than ever, still drivable, one of those derelict cars you see outside a 7-11 after midnight. And eventually things will simply end. Peter out. My guess is that it knows this too.

Here's what else I hope it knows. That its value — and our gratitude for what it does — are light years out in front of the garage queens of its sister cars. That without the Mazda they would not be possible. Nor this business, this house, this dining room table, this feast where we acknowledge what we're blessed with.

Mojo for Christmas

"You finally need to tell me what you want."

Less than a week to go. We're in the basement wrapping ten thousand grandkid presents and she's been after me for days. I run through the things I want that I don't already have. Nothing's missing. It's all there.

"I keep saying. Nothing."

"I'm serious. I need to know now, or it won't get here in time."

To have a year off from Christmas. To have it moved permanently to February 29th. But she's already said no to that.

"I can't think of anything," I say. "Honest."

"Nothing for the Speedster."

"Nothing we could afford."

"Okay," she says finally. "Then I don't want anything either."

Our big furnace room converted to a belly dance studio. All the junk cleared out, a laminate dance floor, wall mirrors, colored stage lights up in the rafters, a sound system. It's all set up, ready to go, all secured with non-refundable deposits. I watch her write "Sophie" on a name tag.

"Wait," I say. "I think I thought of something."

"Well, why don't you tell me."

Building a car and writing a novel have about as much in common, on the surface, as playing a video game and braiding a rug. But there are deep similarities. They both start out as this dream, visionary and compelling, this leap of yearning and imagination. They both qualify as a project. No, not the origami peacock your kid needs for school, but a real project, one that demands serious time and work, an immunity to solitude and frustration, and a deep tank of this high-octane blend of enthusiasm, savagery, dedication, staying power. What we call mojo. Which raises another similarity. Risk. The risk that if you don't attack it hard, and often, you'll never get it done. One day the pickup line in the mojo tank starts sucking air. The project reduces itself to work. Bleak nagging miserable discouraging work. Becomes something you're always meaning to get back to. Goes from the reason your friends used to drop by the house, to a standing joke, to the elephant in the garage that nobody talks about, to the reason your friends no longer call. And then, on a day you can't put your finger on, people have started giving you that sweet "old person" smile. The kind where you look back over your shoulder to see if you parked in a handicapped stall. You didn't. It's just that "unfinished" thing, all over you, like dog hair on black velour.

I started writing a novel eight years ago — about a kid with a used trumpet and a beat-up Porsche — the way most of us build cars. By stealing time from around the edges of my day gig. A snatch of an hour, two, four, sometimes six. Just long enough each time to write a scene. Scenes, I figured, were the fenders and brakes and lights and seats of a novel. I used a spare upstairs bedroom. Wrote when I could. After seven years I had a hundred and sixty scenes. It was assembly time. The news was grim. I'd written the automotive equivalent of seven left front fenders, twelve right side rocker panels, three hoods, thirty-seven taillights. Still missing? Right front fender, left side rocker panel, trunk lid, headlights, a host of other parts. No chassis. No wiring harness. The problem was this. I'd never taken the long stretch of time and distance necessary — Interstate 80 across Nebraska comes to mind — to stand back and see how things were shaping up. The way Jim Michaud and Chip Foose work. Toni saw the problem. I needed to do Nebraska. She told me to go upstairs, full time, to get it done. She'd tend to the business.

Since then I've built a chassis, made most of the missing pieces, started running wires. But the mojo tank was empty. I was climbing the stairs on dread. Inside the door to the room was worse than Mrs. Bates and the portrait of Dorian Gray and Frankenstein combined. My character. No. Not this frigging kid again with his used trumpet and his beat-up Porsche. Please. Grow up. Go away. Here's some money. Buy some gas. Go solve your own problems. Go find your own girlfriend. I'm tired. I'm sick. I'm done.

Here's the difference between an unfinished car and an unfinished novel. You can't invite your buddies over, stock up on Carta Blancas, call Domino's, and do a cold pizza lockdown until it's done. Can't bury it out back and then sell the house. Can't leave it parked behind a dumpster or slip it quietly into a river. Can't put it on eBay and have someone like Alan Merklin take it off your hands. *Unfinished novel. No reserve.* Sure, you could take the manuscript, call the shredder truck, chop your hard drive into little pieces, wad them in liverwurst, feed one piece a day to your neighbor's dog. But that's not where it really is. That's just where it showed up once. Its permanent home is your head. No door. No driveway. No way to haul it out of there. So you're stuck with two options. One, you finish it before you die, or two, you die before you finish it.

Toni's writing "Merle" on a gift tag. Waiting for me to tell her what I want.

"Anything to help me get this frigging novel done."

"Like what?"

"I don't know. Something to keep me from watching *Dirty Jobs* and wishing I had a job cleaning skulls or collecting owl vomit instead."

"I remember the owl vomit guy."

"Like a plaque maybe. With some inspirational saying."

Christmas morning. She opens the card I made up about her belly dance studio. She screams and hugs me. Now it's her turn. I'm wondering what the plaque will say. I Love Me. Live to Write, Write to Live. Life is a Mesmiranda of Variegated Penopholies. There is no plaque. The woman I always underestimate has me sit down at my computer instead. Open my e-mail. There's one from a guy named Andy Craig with an audio file attached. She tells me to turn the volume up and open it.

"Goooood Morning Max!!!!!!!!!!!!"

He means me. I sit there spellbound, blasted up against the back of my chair, while this guy introduces himself, then says all this kickass stuff with all the in-your-face attitude of a super juiced NFL coach. And I'm the only guy in the locker room. I look up at Toni when it's over.

"Holy cow," I say.

"Is that what you meant?"

"Yikes."

"I signed you up for a month."

"A month of what?"

"Personalized motivational messages. You get a new one every morning."

"Who is this guy? Why does he know me?"

"Andy. This is what he does. I talked to him." And then, knowing me, she says, "He's really reasonable. He's beyond reasonable. He's just getting started."

Andy Craig. Toni found him by googling "personalized motivation." What he does takes just a minute first thing in the morning. Jolts you with this Robin Williams greeting. Takes you through a quick warm-up. Has you repeat four or five statements he's composed for you. Then sends you on your way with your mojo tank topped off. By statements I don't mean platitudes. By repeat I don't mean mumble. This guy is mojo personified. Take no prisoners mojo. Pumped. On target. It's been a month now. It works. I see the kid with the used trumpet and the beat-up Porsche the way I first did eight years ago. Fresh. Brand new. The way you'll have a stranger walk up to your finished car and see it the way you first imagined it. Worth building. Worth finishing. Worth taking the distance.

Ghost Riders

I'm no good when it comes to web groups. Drawn way too read-ily to the dark side where the provocateurs, the antagonists, the needlers, the sociopaths, the other misfits hang out. Take things way too much to heart. Get pulled way too quick into those OCD key-board battles where you start out hurt and outraged and indignant and end up confronting the fact that fighting with keyboards is about as feeble an exercise as jacking up a Peterbilt with a paper clip. Which is why, after giving it a longer try than was good for me, I limit myself to lurking, post only rarely and then run like hell, and no longer wake up cotton mouthed with hives, palpitations, sweats, cold sores, numb arms, and my hair on fire because a month ago someone who should never have mattered to me made a gratuitous crack about my horn button. Which is also why I stand in such awe of the people who know enough to stay on the sunny side of the cy-berstreet. Who see the potential for positive good that exists in the very concept of a web group. And then put it to use. Bruce Stumpp is one of these people.

No. I don't know why Stumpp has to end with an extra P any more than I know why Lloyd needs an extra L to get started. But here's what I do know. Back in the early 90s Bruce and his wife Norma, who live in Maryland, bought and built a CMC Speedster. They started cruising. And then they confronted what we all do: the yearning for other like-minded crazies to run with. It wasn't a fruitful hunt. For almost twelve years they roamed the seaboard states looking for ride buddies. At Carlisle they'd see two or three Speedsters. They'd also see the legion of Cobras from the Capitol Area Club. It killed them. Carlisle was the Nationals. It had the whole east coast as a Speedster watershed. There just had to be more. Then, somewhere early in 2003, Bruce found speedsterowners.com, a web group created and hosted by an enterprising and courageous young guy named Theron out in California. A huge site. A global village of Speedsters, owners, aficionados, builders, parts vendors. The Promised Land. The years in the wilderness were over.

Put starkly, speedsterowners.com is like any other web group, a screen of disembodied voices. Aside from their sharply drawn and creative interest in Speedsters, their jokes and stories, and their spelling issues, the rest of who and what they are is nebulous, sketchy, almost ghostlike. It takes guys like Bruce to look at this screen and see what it could be. Real people who don't have a good excuse not to get together. And so it was in August that he started advocating an East Coast Speedster Meet for the 2004 Carlisle Nationals.

There was another Bruce on the group, from the other side of the country, organizing a similar assault on the 2004 Knotts show. They dubbed themselves West Coast Bruce and East Coast Bruce to keep people from getting mixed up and heading the wrong way once they got to I-70 or I-80. East Coast Bruce had a couple of added challenges. The first was the east coast weather in the spring: fickle, erratic, given to random fits of psychopathic sadistic nastiness. The Carlisle translation of Fun in the Sun is Pain in the Rain. The second challenge was a much sparser per capita Speedster population here in the east compared to year-round top-down California, forcing East Coast Bruce to cast a net over the eastern half of the continent to get anywhere near the same catch.

Casting that large a net — and actually netting anyone — called for Bruce to make Carlisle irresistible. Irresistible enough to get people to overcome their instinctual aversion to driving vulnerable little no-see-um cars with the weather protection of outdoor shower stalls across vast potentially cold and stormy distances. To get them to silence their hard-won sense of reason and do something pretty much insane. Other guys stepped up to help with hotel rooms, seminars, hats, drives, awards for longest distances driven and trailered, and other things to do once the only thing left to do was wander around a soggy field looking at Saabs and Fieros. He raised money. Talked Norma into making a couple of giveaway car blankets. His bugle call was drive 'em, trailer 'em, tow 'em, but get 'em there somehow.

In the end it wasn't all the trappings. It was that Bruce's inexhaustible passion and enthusiasm for getting everyone together took on the contagious draw of Max Yasgur's farm in Woodstock. Yeah. Let's find out if we're who we say we are. If we're not just brains in jars in front of telekinetic keyboards. If Hoss really does drive his Subie Cabriolet wearing a ten-gallon hat. If Tony Carrer really does have a salmon-colored Speedster with black catpaws painted up across its nose. If there really is a guy from Jersey with the awesome name of Herbert Kruttschnitt III. If Gordon's CMC is really Pearl. If. If. If. The magnetic pull of the possibility of cyberpeople becoming manifest enough to shake hands and have a beer with. This was what got over fifty Speedsters to Carlisle, from places like Canada, Florida, Iowa, New England, Tennessee, the Virginias and Carolinas, Ohio.

Bruce is as unassuming as they come. When you ask him how he did it, he'll be evasive about his own effort, and talk instead about the people who helped him. So I'll let him have his way. Rocky Cimbrec doing liaison duty with the New Jersey Replicar Club to give the Speedster guys an introductory first-year place to land. Alan Merklin taking care of hotel and dinner accommodations. Bill Drayer mapping out drives around the area. Barry Fuchs creating a website dedicated to the meet. Gordon Nichols tackling the logistics of getting people there, organizing interstate caravans from all directions, bringing a trailer full of tools and parts. But when you talk to these guys, all of them will point you back to Bruce.

That original three-day party has become an annual event, expanded to include Spyders, extended to four days. Last year Bruce handed it off to Gordon Nichols. Gordon — another first class guy — took it to the next level with an actual on-site Speedster build. The contagion has fired up more vendor interest too. And the impact has rippled beyond Carlisle. According to Norma, people took friendships home with them, and the East Coast now has a real community of Speedster owners who know where to find each other.

We've all seen the movie. A farmer builds a ballpark in his cornfield and then waits to see who'll wander out of the corn. At the awards dinner that first year, Bruce stood in front of the roomful of men and women he'd brought together, tried to thank them, and choked up. I sat there watching him wrestle with feelings I imagined were overwhelming. I wondered if my favorite moment was on his mind. The moment where he and Norma are standing there, that first afternoon at Carlisle, all the hard work done, everything prepared, waiting to see how their effort would materialize. The first sighting. Small trembling ephemeral ripples of red and pearl and silver and black and blue and white and green and salmon, shimmering out there on the concrete horizon of I-81, the distant growling mutter coming and going and coming again on the wind. Slow to take on form and substance. Then coming down the offramp. Swinging into the hotel parking lot. Speedsters. Convertible Ds. Cabriolets. Spyders. Guys and gals. Ghost Riders from across the ragged skies of cyberspace. Everything coming real.

Fiero Rising

Last year, looking to amp up the thrill of the replica-import nationals beyond the usual out-of-the-rain seminars, dyno runs, egg-and-ham sandwiches, and the scariest flea market this side of the Westminster Dog Show, the Carlisle folks put out a call for new ideas. Harold Pace came up with doing something on the order of the Burning Man thing in Nevada. He'd been there. Had a photo album of the topless bike ride they get the women to do. The Carlisle folks jumped on the concept.

So this year there's this lone little red Fiero, sitting there in the middle of the show field, all by itself in a clearing about a hundred feet around. From there to the back reaches of the field are all the usual Carlisle suspects. This being the year "Carlisle Celebrates The Volvo," there's thousands of them, row after row, the parking lot of a Swedish Wal-Mart. I'm on my way to interview the Fiero, but here's this guy who dusted off his Volvo, cracked the hood, then took up vigil next to it, waiting for me to come along. Eye contact. I'm done.

"Hi," I say. "I'm Billy."

"Hi. I'm Paul."

I love the way people with name tags forget how you already know who they are.

"Nice car. How much safety does it put out?"

"Oh, around twelve thousand. Haven't rated it lately."

I ask him don't you have to wreck it to rate it. This ripple of a dubious smile before he tells me there are theoretical ways. Says he's got it up to forty-three air bags. Gearshift, radio knobs, door handles, cup holders, vanity mirrors. Pretty much everything's bagged. All full flow bags. Xenon brake lights, school zone detector, breakaway bike rack, chipped seat belt ratchets, drilled out crumple zone, ignition lockout to test your breath for meat. I ask him if it can tell meat from cheese. For sure, he says, fish too. Chardonnay from Blue Nun.

"I'm getting a rev limiter that holds it to 45 rpm," he says.

"Cool."

Questions I want to ask the little red Fiero. Why they show up at all at the replica and import nationals. If they're actually replicas of 914s or some forgotten Fiat. Or if they qualify as imports because Pontiac was owned by Skoda while they were in production. Or if they're just tired of living. Looking to be euthanized by someone who bought himself a Lambo kit. All Saturday I keep meaning to get out to where it sits. But the distractions keep coming. I meet a young guy named Cory Drake who's got the most amazingly innovative self-designed home-built race-prepped Speedster I've ever seen. He lets Rocky and me take it out for this rawboned lunatic ride through the countryside. When we get back I'm pumped. In this mood to keep borrowing other people's stuff. Hoping Johnny Hallstrand will let me wear his ten-gallon hat. Bob Hess will let me use the back seat of his EasyRods 49 Ford to show Toni where babies used to come from. Chuck Beck will let me borrow his 904 until my funeral. Wild Bill Drayer will let me use his face to give out Jeff Bridges autographs. Paul will let me safety test his Volvo the real way. Dave Betts will loan me his 427 Cobra to teach the kids in my neighborhood what streets are really for. John Steele will sell me a 356 coupe for a dollar a year for twenty thousand years. Chuck Siewert will let Toni and me take Carolyn's T-Bird out to the Dairy Queen.

"You're mean," Chuck says, when Toni asks, because the standing joke all weekend has been that he didn't get it done in time for Carlisle.

By Saturday night, I've missed a hundred chances to interview the little red Fiero, and now, at dusk, gathered around it with Boss Jim and the rest of the KCB staff, it's too late. Rich Lacy has his big Classic Transport rig backed out onto the grass. Jim's holding this big remote control box. He pushes a button. The Fiero shudders, just once, lifts off of its wheels, then rises off the grass on this hoist. It passes the high enough to work under mark. I expect it to stop. But the big steel shaft keeps coming up out of the grass. I've seen this before, I realize, but it was a beanstalk, and it was in a movie. Soon the hoist is flagpole high. It keeps pushing, pushing the little Fiero higher, up out of the shadow of the field to where it catches sunlight. It finally stops with this quick hydraulic snort. It has to be ten stories up, high as the top of a redwood fired by the sunset, swaying against the slow immense passage of Carlisle's usual armada of huge clouds. We're surrounded by this ring of a thousand Volvos, fender to fender, and out behind the Volvos, people, shoulder to shoulder, sunburned heads like a migrant's dream of endless red cabbages out across the deep shadows of the field and up into the light fading off the hills.

Jim lines us up in this bucket brigade between the trailer and the hoist. Rich starts handing down Duraflame logs, we start handing them along, Jim starts stacking them around the hoist. I'm handing them off to Steve Temple.

"You could build a house with all these logs."

"You couldn't afford the fire insurance," Steve says.

I remember Cory telling me that after doing the Navy he became a firefighter.

"Maybe fire departments build practice houses out of them."

"I'd like to do that bike ride story."

Rich gets the trailer emptied and takes his hauler out of there. Two Volvos back out to let him through. High up, Jim lays the last of the logs against the shaft, ties them in with duct tape, then uses what's left of the roll to rappel back down. The Fiero's in shadow now. Just this lazy swaying silhouette on its ten-story stem. "Showtime," Jim says. He raises his arm. The ring of Volvos ignites in headlights. Suddenly we're this paralyzed cluster of two-legged deer. From behind the headlights rises this roar of shouting, singing, clapping. Jim frisks his pockets like he's arresting himself. Carolyn tells him he doesn't smoke. I give him my Bic. He sprints around the pile lighting wrappers. This blue flickering halo starts climbing off the logs. Behind it the real flames take hold. The joyous roar of the crowd takes on the awful character of the last thing Custer heard. The fire starts rising out of itself like this monstrous awakening beast. Heat shoves us back. Air bags start popping. Volvos start backing away. Light more blank and pitiless than sunlight lays the field bare. The crowd goes quiet. Church quiet. Sunglasses appear. People up in the hills are hurrying their clothes back on. High above us — trembling at the edge of its kindling point — the bright and tragic undercarriage of the little red Fiero I'll never get to interview.

Forever Young

I love this hobby like I do a deviled egg. For the white but especially the yolk. For the cars but especially the people. People who only left high school because they had to. People whose hearts rejected their diplomas.

I met Rocky the first time I went to a New Jersey Replicar Club meeting. He and Linda were raised in an Adirondacks town called Saranac Lake in upstate New York well north of Albany. It's a typical snowbelt town, a small downtown heart of strong old wintered buildings, a bar every three feet to keep people from getting lost in the snow dunes, and roads that were intuitively engineered to go the way a drunk would expect them to. Lake Placid is a hop away. Every February Rocky and Linda head home for a reunion. A few years back they invited us along.

Long ago, I spent two years in a college town north of Syracuse, on Lake Ontario, where the locals complained that if the Erie Canal hadn't been built, this broke little town with 192 bars and 25 annual feet of snow would be Chicago. I came to love the upstate concept.

That much snow, that many bars, the total abdication to salt eating out your fenders, just makes you stupid. High school stupid. In Saranac Lake I found that concept waiting. Snowbanks made festive with beer cups and blood. Guys too drunk to know the blood was theirs or their date was their brother's wife. Anything can be ventured. Anything forgiven. That night we went to hear a band we know from Jersey, Big Boss Sausage and the Missing Links, where a kid reeled around the floor like a punchdrunk boxer, taking every drum beat like an uppercut. In the morning Rocky brought up this bobsled ride in Lake Placid. I looked at his Spanky from the Little Rascals grin and said yeah.

The ticket shack sells two rides. One's a mile long, runs a hundred twenty five a head, uses this big new overhead track that Olympians train on. You can see its long underbelly, this tube the size of the Lincoln Tunnel up on struts, looping down the mountain like some Jules Verne serpent. The other ride is thirty bucks, half a mile, and uses the run that was built for the 62 Olympics. Sixty bucks lighter, Rocky and me start the climb up the mountain along the run. It's this twisting ice-coated concrete trench cut down the mountain like a storm canal. Steep. Deep. Quiet. Suddenly this voice comes blasting out of speakers hidden in the woods like snipers. *They're through the little esses . . . they're ziggin' . . . they're zaggin' . . . they're on the straight . . .* And then this sled comes slamming down the trench, this raging bull of a red torpedo, five helmets huddled in a row behind its battered nose. And then it's gone. There were people in there. People. I look at Rocky. Wonder if my own grin looks nuts too.

We make the top. A guy picks two scarred helmets off a rack for us. The sled is old enough to have figured out that hell is a state of life. The driver points us into position. Rocky first. Me next. Two more pack in behind me. I'm tucked up so tight behind Rocky that if I pee my pants, his will get wet first, and if the guy behind me goes, I'll be the first to know. Then we're off. We're doin' the little esses and then we're ziggin' and we're zaggin' but we don't hear the speakers telling us this time. This is like riding the crooked funnel of the devil's personal chauffeur-driven twister. You're getting rocketed and slammed up walls and then down and across and up again so fast you don't know how to pay attention. Like divorce, or throwing up, there's nothing you can do but let it happen. Inside your helmet, you're hollering, laughing, screaming, absurd with terror. Then it's over. Up a runaway lane, on snow, a rooster tail off the brake. Sixty-five miles an hour down a gash in the mountain so narrow you could step across it with a walker. It's absurd to be alive. Rocky's got a long burn in his parka through to his sweatshirt sleeve. Musta hit the wall, he says. Shrugs. And then we're laughing, laughing like there's no tomorrow, because both of us know there shouldn't be. I can see it in the whites of Rocky's eyes.

We head back to Saranac Lake, hook up with Linda and Toni at a restaurant, raise a toast to the women, to us for holding on to them, to Rocky's arm-saving parka, and it goes on and on, to lettuce, to topsoil, to whoever invented shrubs, and I finally ask the waiter for the check. He hands me back my Visa card. Cash only. I ask Rocky to drive me to an ATM. It's dark outside. Raining. The parking lot is this moonscape of winter ice and puddles the size of wading pools. Suddenly Rocky's gone. I look around. Hear laughing. Look down. There he is, on his back, in six inches of black water, a human island. I get him to his feet. And then I go. And somehow that sets us off. We get laughing so hard we can't stop. All the way to the bank we keep lighting each other off. Rocky stops just back of the ATM. I get out and go to put my card in. It doesn't go. I turn it every way I can. Won't happen. Figuring it's an upstate ATM, and might need a drink first, I look through the windshield for Rocky. He's useless. Just watching me has got him banging his head on the steering wheel. I check out the card I'm holding. It says *Comfort Inn*. I've gotta stagger back and share my imbecility with Rocky. This time he gets laughing so hard he has to get out and do a body slam into a snowbank.

Back at the restaurant, still giggling like we've taken Tuesday off the map, I pay the waiter, take a stool at the bar. The local next to me buys me a shot of something called Yukon Jack. Linda says to watch it. Says it's like truth serum. Says they call it Yukon Talk. I ask my new friend what he does. He downs his shot. Tells me how he works in this bodyshop. How once upon a time he owned it. How his brother worked for him. How somewhere along the way he started a thing with his brother's wife. How his brother caught on. How he made amends by giving his brother the shop. How suddenly he found himself unemployed. How his brother, out of brotherly love, offered him a job in the shop he used to own. Where he used to be his brother's boss.

We watch the barmaid do a rye and coke. I'm amazed that I'm drunk enough to have followed him. And then he wants to know what I do. I take a long considered look at my untouched shot of Yukon Talk. Upstate. Anything can be forgiven. I pick it up, slug it down, get started.

Amazing Grace

At the VFW hall, people sit at round fold-away tables arranged around three walls of a large room with a hardwood floor, no-frills chandeliers, a small cash bar at the far end with a framed quilt of the American flag up on the wall behind it. I'm at the bar with Charlie. Charlie's there because he runs the place, rents it out, tends the bar. I'm there because my wife Toni is a Champagne Girl, a member of a bellydancing troupe that does performances for charity, and the troupe's performing tonight to raise money for a shelter. I typically see Charlie once a year because the New Jersey Replicar Club holds its annual winter banquet here. By coincidence, the Champagne Girls rent the same hall for some of their performances.

By coincidence too, Charlie's an old Porsche guy. He came back from Vietnam and bought himself an old 356 coupe. He's seen my Speedster. I've tried talking him into building himself one. Naw, he says, he likes to leave things where they happened. Tonight I'm pushing Charlie again. Telling him about this guy John Steele who's building a replica of his old coupe. It perks him up good for a minute. Out on the floor, a dance number's ending, people are clapping, cameras are going. Charlie says tell him more. I keep going. Hold it, he says, watch this. A woman comes through the tables out to the center of the open floor. She's barefoot, dressed in a long low-riding colored skirt, a sparkling beaded belt and beaded brassiere, tiny gold cymbals in her fingers. Somewhere in her thirties, strong without looking muscular, her skin this honey tan, long tight midriff, loose brown hair with rich threads of summer honey in it. She sets a long curved sword across her head, finds its balance point, lets go. Sitar music starts playing. The sword stays remarkably still while she does this slow and sinuous dance underneath it. And then, still dancing, the cymbals in her fingers ringing, she starts leaning back, slowly letting her knees give, the sword on her head like a limbo stick she can't disturb. Her skirt falls open off her legs. Against all the laws of physics as I know them, she keeps going, deeper and deeper, until her shoulders touch the floor, and then her back, and for a minute she dances there in that position, almost prone, mostly with her arms, the sword still on her head. And then, still dancing, she starts rising, first from her shoulders, then from her back and waist, and finally from her knees, this fluid rising motion until she's erect again, on her feet. All without hands. No sign of the strength it took or the hundreds of muscles she had to orchestrate. All with a sword on her head so remarkably still it looked like it was sleeping. It's one of the most amazing athletic feats I've ever seen.

Everyone claps. I look at Charlie. He gives me this nod that says I told you. We start watching the next dance. In a couple of minutes a woman shows up at the bar. She's in a raincoat. Charlie knows her. Rum and coke? he says. Yup, she says. Asks him how he's been. They chat for a minute. And then she's talking to me.

"So what'd you think?"

I look at her. No smile. Just this frank question in her still face. It takes me a minute. She's not as tall up close as she was out on the floor, but where her raincoat's open, I can see the glittering beadwork of her bra and belt, her feet bare.

"The sword. That was you."

"Yeah."

"It was unbelievable."

Her name is Sharon. She lives in Bayonne with her husband and three boys. Aside from charity dancing, she teaches a bellydancing course at Rutgers, does "bellygrams" for Christmas cash. She loves the shore. At some point she tells me she's a pipefitter. It catches me off guard. I'm used to seeing women work construction sites, but having just watched her dance, it's hard to go the distance to coveralls and a welder's helmet. We start talking power plants. She's been on the scrubber at Mercer and the repower project at Linden. I've written safety standards she's had to work to. I don't recall how we got to 9/11. Maybe because it was that time of year, as it is now, and it was in the news.

That morning, she and her crew were replacing the air handling system on the roof of an eight-story building on the Hoboken waterfront, across the Hudson just north of the end of Manhattan and the shining boxes of the Towers. The first plane came down the river and over their heads so low she ducked. In the noise and wind of the jet wash she turned in time to see it knife through the wall of the North Tower and the fireball blow out the other side. The upper floors were laying their plume of smoke out over Brooklyn toward the southeast reaches of Queens and Jamaica Bay when the second plane hit the second tower. She saw people fall from windows. She saw the South Tower and then the North Tower come down. At the bar she tells Charlie and me how you could hear each floor break loose. She gives us the sound — *chick chick chick chick chick chick* — and uses her hand to make small descending chops in the air. Soon after, her crew was ordered downstairs, and a police boat took them across the river. She spent every day of the next three months at Ground Zero.

She tells this story, five years in her past, in the plain and spare and economic way you hear construction workers talk. Charlie asks how she's doing. We both know what he's asking because it's been in the news too. How they're getting sick. She tells us she's getting regular testing but nobody can tell her anything. She can't push herself like she did. Gets this cough when she works outside in winter. Comes home at night to her boys so tired sometimes her husband has to tend to them. Who knows what slow poisons nested in her lungs that first day, in the smoke and dust, and then for the next three months, while she worked shoulder to shoulder with other unprotected workers, taking that terrible mountain down. She knows she was hurt. Just not how deep it goes or how long it could take to know. In the way she talks there's nothing close to pity. It's just a different sword. One she's still learning how to balance.

A year from this night, John's replica of Charlie's old coupe will have come to life, and appeared in this magazine, in an issue I'll hold until the next time I see him. For now, Toni's on the floor, doing her own solo, where she dances behind a half transparent veil she holds like a quivering curtain in front of herself, then drops when the number ends. I watch it fall, leave her standing there, her own scant costume shimmering.

2008

Frank and Me

I've got a friend in Pennsylvania named Frank. No, he's not a friend I went out and made myself, like Alan or Tim or Bill or Rocky or Wade. Frank's the friend the Pennsylvania DMV assigned to me when I called them on the promise they used to put on their license plates. They recently stopped honoring that promise and took the slogan off their plates. But I managed to get Frank grandfathered. That means he always has to be my Friend in Pennsylvania. It doesn't mean he has to shine my shoes or buy my groceries or send his wife to my igloo. Just be my State Friend.

He owns a Brubaker Box. He lives in a gray house. A kit car and a gray house were two of the preferences I listed when I filled out my Friend in Pennsylvania application. I didn't get everything I asked for — like female — but I'm okay with Frank. He's short and porky, shaves his head, keeps one of his fingernails long to pick his left ear with, and thinks George Carlin's hypothetical questions are supposed to have answers. Like most car guys he's a solid driver. Takes particular pride in his left turns. One night we stumble into this argument between driving being a right or a privilege. It's Cruise Night, we're sitting in his Box, washing down onion rings with Rolling Rocks.

I see it like this. Driving was a privilege back when I was four or five and asked my dad if I could borrow the Valiant wagon for a date. It was his car. His insurance. His gas. His milk crate I sat on. His golf club I used to reach the pedals. His taxes that paid for the roads I'd use. His butt that got called if I took my kindergarten sweetie home with the ribbon in her hair crooked. When my dad said yes, and handed me the keys, I knew I was being extended a privilege.

I'm all grown up now. I buy my own car. My own insurance. My own gas. I pay for the roads I use. I pay the salary of every civil servant who works for the DMV and its black hole of courts and police and road departments. And they want to tell me that they're extending me a privilege by allowing me to drive. Right. Like having your housecleaner allow you to live in your house. Hey. Take your Tilex and go. Don't let your Swiffer hit you in the rear.

Frank takes the high road. "Driving is a privilege of civil society which an individual committing offenses against that society forfeits." He recites it like it's scripture. I feel like I'm being sacrilegious when I ask him what kinds of offenses. And then his high road hits a downgrade. For Frank, offenses cover anything that gets in the way of his Box, or doesn't jibe with his personal road code. A Buick doing a mile under the speed limit. A Volvo with its baked-out paint shingled with peace stickers. A ratty Honda with a widemouth exhaust and a Domino sign on the roof. "It's a privilege, you effin' stupid turkey baster! Remember that!"

"You're a road bigot, Frank."

"Why do you say that?"

Because I can. Because under the old Friend in Pennsylvania statute, they give you a lot of latitude on what you can say to your grandfathered friend.

"Not everybody can cut a left the way you do," I say. "They still got a right to the road. They paid their way. Just like you."

He picks his ear. It's Carlin time. Like it always is when I stump him. "Why don't sheep shrink in the rain?" he says.

"They do," I tell him.

My real problem with the word "privilege" is this. It's a lot easier to take away a privilege than a right. You can't mess around with a right. You've got to go by the book. You can get real capricious with a privilege. And that's what's happening. License suspensions are catching on as the national penalty of choice for offenses with no relation to driving. I remember when the penalty for graffiti was dipping your tongue in turpentine and licking Suzy's name off the wall. For underage smoking it was throwing up. For buying a high school girl a pack of Chesterfields it was 30 cents. For skipping school it was watching your buddies graduate. For not supporting your kids it was a vasectomy with a weed whacker. For doing a doobie it was spending four hours in front of the candy rack at the minimart wondering what it was you walked over here to get. These days? Poof. Your license is gone. And then your job. And then whatever depended on your having one. Like child support.

"I gotta go," says Frank. "You're gonna have to let me out."

I keep forgetting his Box only has the one door. A big slider. On the passenger side. I'm seized with this feeling of unbelievable power. Like having the emergency exit seat on a plane when there's finally an emergency. I give myself a minute to savor it. "My privilege," I finally tell him.

I'm not soft on driving. Not by a long shot. In the driver's seat in a moving vehicle you do one thing. Drive. That's it. Anything else should be illegal. But it comes down to this. The reason you lose your license has to have something to do with driving. Getting behind the wheel so drunk you punch twenty holes through your steering column looking for the ignition slot? Using your grandkids for pylons to set up a parking lot slalom? Yeah. You need your license yanked. But smoking? Using a wall to tell Suzy you love her? This is what happens when you downgrade a right to a privilege. It's open season. Failure to wear your Broncos cap every other Tuesday. Frank's back from the head. "I still say it's a privilege," he says.

"Try telling your NRA buddies that having a gun is a privilege."

Frank looks at something he just picked out of his ear. "I heard that cannibals don't eat clowns because they taste funny," he says.

"It's not true."

Two kids are at his window. One wants to know if his Box is a life-size Hot Wheels. The other kid wants to know if we're gay. It's time to go. The next time I see him he tells me he's painted his house red. I report him to the Friend in Pennsylvania hotline. A week later he calls me. Says they just yanked his license for a year. He's desperate. He can't do his paper route. So he can't pay his child support.

"What's my house color got to do with my driver's license?"

Another hypothetical question he thinks is supposed to have an answer. So I give him one. Not a thing.

Road Deprivation Disorder

I built my car to drive it. It was done the day I got it the way Toni wanted it. My mechanic Wade and I still periodically hanker for converting it to a five-speed IRS. In the meantime I drive it. Take it out an hour or two ahead of sunset, clear a couple of towns, and I'm among the farms and woods and hills of the mostly unmolested Delaware River region, following roads that meander and snake and lift and fall through some of the loveliest country I know, getting and staying lost, chasing horizons, escaping everything that has a name I recognize. I come home at sunset as blank and imbecilic as a brand new baby, purified by wind and light and Santana, and make Toni guess what my name is. The bad news is that I only get to do this on a seasonal basis. The rest of the year — the dark hard stubborn months from November back again to April — it takes pills to approach the same experience.

SAD. Someone named it seasonal affective disorder in order to give it that clever acronym. One of its causes is light deprivation. Its symptoms include excessive sleeping, lack of energy, carbohydrate craving, mood depression, hopelessness, suicidal thinking, decreased self esteem, social withdrawal. But SAD isn't just a human phenomenon. It cuts across nature. Excessive sleeping? Bears give in and hibernate. Decreased self-esteem? Put yourself in the shoes of a tree and imagine going hairless every fall. Suicidal thinking? Flowers and insects just up and kill themselves. Light deprivation? Birds chase it south. SAD is nature. Every living thing gives in to it. Only humans call it a disorder. Only humans make it worse by throwing Christmas in the mix.

But there's one strain of SAD that is distinctly manmade, and exclusively human, and affects a small but vital subset of the population. Us. Those of us who build and drive to stay off drugs. Who know that "season" has a meaning other than shaking tabasco into a taco. I recently sat down with Dr. Kit Car to discuss this human-specific strain. He calls it road deprivation disorder. RDD. No clever acronym. Just what it is. It begins with the onset of road deprivation season. RDS.

RDS, like its light deprivation counterpart, typically begins in late fall and runs to early spring. Your personal RDS depends on the latitude of your neighborhood. The average RDS for Kansas, for example, is shorter than what they get in Canada. It also depends on the kind of car you drive — hardtop or convertible — and the BTU rating of its heater. Some of us try to eliminate RDS altogether by doing the year-round thing in a closed and heated car. It depends too on how we mark the onset and ending of RDS. Those of us who lean toward being social mark the season from the last cruise night in the fall to the first one the following spring. Those of us who like chasing the sunset mark our RDS from the day they yank Daylight Savings Time to the day they restore it again. Those of us with flared rear fenders — us Cobra, Diva, Lotus, and widebody Speedster folks — know what road grit means. RDS begins, for us, the first day the sanding truck goes past the house, and doesn't end until the sweeper truck makes its passes up and down the road.

RDD shares all the symptoms of SAD but adds a few of its own. My friend Roger sits in his driveway in a lawn chair every Friday off the back of his covered Valkyrie. My friend Dave sets up a cardboard cutout of your typical Cobra admirer in his garage and spends hours answering his questions. My friend John makes hangup calls on Harold Pace. My friend Andy keeps showing up at the police station confessing to the suicide bombing of his Diablo. My friend Alan finds some wormhole in the Internet and comes back a week later, a thousand years older but no less miserable, with some of the weirdest video clips this side of the Horsehead Nebula. Frank, my State Friend in Pennsylvania, hits out-of-the-way mini-marts and switches the bottlecaps on all the Mountain Dews and Dr. Peppers in the coolers.

I know guys who try to beat RDD by planning "winter projects" for their cars. I know other guys who go the other way — the way of denial — and pursue "winter hobbies" instead. Learn how to play the accordion. Whittle flutes and whistles out of hambones from Thanksgiving. Stuff and mount the koi they forgot to feed.

During our interview I asked Dr. Kit Car whether RDD sufferers can hope for a cure sometime in the near future. He said that the only known cure at this time is to eliminate its root cause. Road deprivation. Give yourself year-round access to the road. Move closer to the equator. Or, short of finding that possible, wait for global warming to come to your neighborhood. Global warming, he said, will gradually reverse the current demographic of RDD, affecting low-lying coastal areas as opposed to northern climates. One cure for those folks, he says, might be ark building.

In the meantime, as I write this at the tail end of January, I've turned the big corner and can look ahead to where RDS will pretty much be over for the year. But Dr. Kit Car advises caution. The disorder doesn't end, he says, when the season does. There are consequences to four or five or six months of road deprivation. When it comes to RDD, we're still psychologically Newtonian, still governed by the law of equal and opposing forces. RDD is a psychic trampoline. What goes down must come up. The deeper you go into the "down" symptoms — lethargy and despair and suicidal brooding — the higher your rebound into the "up" symptoms — hypomania and mania. Folks on the upside of RDD are energetic, euphoric, brimming with new ideas, confident, charismatic, immune to fear, doubt, or social inhibition. They talk readily to strangers, offer unsolicited solutions to their problems, take inordinate pleasure in little things. Other symptoms to look for are rapid speech, directionless high-speed thinking, late-night drinking, and grandiosity.

Sound familiar? No, you won't see this kind of behavior at Knotts, because RDD won't come to Knotts until global warming turns Los Angeles into Atlantis. But think Carlisle. Why else would everyone look so thrilled to spend three days in the rain? Why else would Paul act like he's got a lifetime subscription to Rodney Dangerfield running in his head? Why else would Doug find cigarette butts in the gravel hilarious? Why else would Lane come back from the flea market with the left fender to a 1948 Renault? What else would make people bring their Volvos? And are the Carlisle Marching Band's ham and egg sandwiches really worth the drive from Ontario?

The folks who come to Carlisle from down south — another demographic that doesn't know RDD from regional demolition derby—stand around wondering what the big deal is. Some of them get nervous. Like they've been excluded from some cosmic joke. Others get scared. "Last time a guy from Jersey was that excited to show me his Cobra," says Tom, "he was wearing pink cowboy boots." I dedicate this story to you unsuspecting folks. You're not being left out. This May, at Carlisle, just try to understand the high the rest of us are on. See you there.

Some People Collect Art

Crazy Bill the retired Continental pilot is there with the motor home he rented, parked in one of the coveted spots along the back stretch just before the bus stop, and Jerry and his gal are there, and Tommy, and Richard, and Mark and Jane, along with Toni and me. We're sitting outside the motor home, in the dark, in a variety of folding chairs around a smoking patch of dirt with an occasional flicker of blue flame, and the bickering starts because we're all from Jersey, all adults, all proud members of the New Jersey Replicar Club, and not one of us can get a fire started, even though we've got Duraflames for firewood and gasoline for kindling.

"I get warmer watching the Yule Log," says Tommy.

"I get warmer reading a Hallmark card," says Jerry.

Meanwhile, four campsites over, there's a group of three guys from Rochester, and they've got a fire going that Joan of Arc would die all over for. You can see their shoes and teeth and beer cans glowing. Hear them telling jokes, laughing, while we're sitting in the dark, shivering, bickering away. We need to mooch some real firewood. More than that. We need to mooch the aptitude for what to do with it. Bill wants Toni to do the mooching because one of the Rochester guys has the hots for her. He's asked her ten times that day if she's got a sister. Jerry calls Bill a pimp and tells him to do his own mooching. Mark says try offering them a case of beer. Jane says we're down to two cans. Richard says to tell them we can pay them back tomorrow from the firewood place just down the road.

"I don't see how you can build a Daytona and not know how to build a fire," Tommy says to Bill.

Not only a Daytona. But two Cobras before that. Not only build. Bill's raced all three of them, on tracks from Loudon to Lime Rock to Pocono to where we are now, The Glen, on a Friday in September, at the end of Day One of the Zippo Vintage Grand Prix. And not just Bill. We've all built cars. Mark an MG. Jerry a Jaguar. Tommy an Allard. Richard a GT40. Me a Speedster. We've spent the day watching every car sanctioned by the Sportscar Vintage Racing Association (SVRA) race this historic track that runs more than three miles up and down the hills and through the woods of western New York State. Ten or eleven different groups. We've been to all our favorite watching spots around the track. The hill down into the boot with the hard left-hander at the bottom. The toe of the boot where you can sit on the rise and watch cars come screaming sideways around the carousel of the hairpin. The bus stop where cars come off the asphalt bumpers on two wheels in these howling fishtails and go roaring out the other end. The esses. The grandstands. We've wandered through the garages and around the paddocks. Talked to drivers and mechanics. Seen everything. Sprites, Minis, MGAs, Lotus 7s. Formula Vees, Brabhams, Merlyns, Elvas. Pre-1972 Triumphs, Porsches, Healeys, Daimlers. Pre-1960 limited and GT cars from Devins and Maseratis to Jags and Listers to Allards and Spyders. GTs and prototypes and Can-Ams from every 900 designation ever used by Porsche to McLarens, Lolas, Chevrons, and GT40s. Pre-war Bugattis, Alfas, Bentleys, Morgans. Pre-1972 musclecars from Vettes to Cobras to Camaros to Mustangs to Cougars and Barracudas. All original. Not parked. Not show field still. But racing. Flat out. After the first day of this three-day weekend, everyone's favorite is this late 60s Camaro, stripped to pure gray primer metal, some wild young guy at the wheel who drives like the suicidal hero of every hot rod movie I remember. He's everyone's favorite because, like most of us, it's just him and his salvaged home-prepped car. Not some seven-figure fantasy. No big decked-out hauler. No hired mechanics. No sponsors. Word has gone around that his biggest rival is another Camaro, jockeyed by some cool hired driver who's being paid 300 grand for the weekend.

The first time I was here — eight years ago — a buddy from down the street who'd been coming to The Glen since its glory days of Formula One suggested we run up. We left at four in the morning on Friday. Four hours later I was standing in brisk morning sunlight on a rise at a shabby wire fence, a beer in my hand, turning down a toke on a doobie, while cars from another century came downshifting off a straightaway, dove into this sweeping turn around me, went howling down a forested hill. In the space of a single day I'd experienced every car I'd ever dreamed of. The next year I brought Toni. And every year since then.

You get wrecks. All of a sudden, four laps into a race, the hills and the woods go quiet. And you make friends. People you know will be here next year, on the same patch of dirt at the bus stop, at the same campsite, at the same table in the Glen Club where you said goodbye a year ago. Rich, the auto parts guy from Connecticut, whose nineties-vintage Audi is closing in on the 400 thousand mile mark. Debi and Jack, from Oswego, a jug of Jaegermeister chilling in their camper fridge. Bob, the retired Kodak engineer, and his son Bob, the aspiring indie filmmaker. And now, three guys from Rochester, four campsites down, the heat of their fire evident in their warm-sounding banter.

Two days from now the guy in the gray primer Camaro will beat out his overpaid nemesis to win the musclecar group. For now it's cold — a fall night — and we've got a campfire problem. Toni finally loses patience with the bickering. Gets up and heads over. A while later she's back. Three guys from Rochester are behind her. One with beer. Two with firewood. I don't want to know the details. I'm hoping it involves some made-up sister.

"You guys ever build a Daytona?" says Bill. Sounding hurt.

The last few years we've introduced the event to other folks in the club. Gordon Nichols (the guy I wish would run for President) has started herding together Speedster Owner guys. The draw is self-evident. This place, on this weekend, is the source for just about every replica we build and drive. Its provenance. Its history. Up close. In action. Ragged and dirty and stinking and busted up and living out its life the way it oughta. Some people collect art. Us folks, we replicate it, improvise on it. The SVRA folks, well, they take it out and race it.

Instead of Carlisle

We had all our reservations made, the car registered, friends expecting us, and then Thursday afternoon, wrapping up business to get out of here early the next day, I started feeling low. When I got up Friday, things down in the Kansas region of my innards were rough, tornadoes highly likely, storm chasers rigging up their cameras, hitting the road. We waited all morning for things to clear at least long enough for the three-hour ride to Carlisle. No luck. Around noon we decided to shut down any hope of going. Called and canceled our reservations, got word to Diamond Geezer that we wouldn't be making the KCB staff dinner that night, called Ohio Bruce and Julie to tell them we'd try again next year, let Gordon know we wouldn't be making the Saturday night dinner, called and told Rocky he'd have to handle the Chippendale's gig we were signed up to do at the All Star Café all by himself. He said it wouldn't work without me there to hold his hat. It hurt like crazy. The first Carlisle in eight or nine years running we couldn't make. From there, facing an empty weekend, rain coming down hard, we hunkered down and wondered how to spend it.

I define genius as the unemployed guy who was watching Divorce Court one afternoon, looked down to find himself twiddling his thumbs, and wondered how he could put that idle activity to work and maybe make some money. What he came up with spawned the socio-economic phenomenon of video games and created a generation of thumb talkers. Both Toni and I were born too soon to catch this cultural wave. So, for the weekend, we had to fall back on more traditional rainy day stuff. We hauled out our battered old board games. For obvious reasons, we passed on Sorry, and all Monopoly did was remind us how broke we were for all the time I'd taken off to write a novel. So, being in an automotive frame of mind already, we came up with building our own little Carlisle. We worked from a Google Earth layout of the show field. Masked and sprayed all the roads in gray primer on the family room floor. Made barns and pavilions out of cardboard. Tents out of upholstery swatches and toothpicks. Gathered all the Hot Wheels our boys had left behind and lined them up. We even mapped out the flea market. Before we got around to figuring what to fill the stalls with, we started talking about how to populate the place, what to use for Hoss Hallstrand's ten gallon hat, who to give Cobra Dave for an audience, how to make miniature ham and egg sandwiches. That was when we hit the wall. All we were doing, we realized, was powering up the heartbreak.

So, from there, we came up with the slightly less masochistic game of Carlisle Hold 'Em. Cut some old card stock we had down to playing card dimensions. Made a Carlisle deck. We had Cobra cards, Speedster cards, MG cards, Lambo cards, GT40 cards, Jag cards, Sebring cards, Willys cards, hot rod cards, Auburn cards, Ferrari cards, Dragon cards, everything. Gave them different brand names. To keep things true to the scope of Carlisle, we threw in some imports, Peugeots, Audis, Bugeyes, Saabs, Volvos, a couple of sacrificial Fieros. Then we started allocating values and making up some rules. Should a Ferrari be a King. Should a Valkyrie be a Jack. Queen was easy — a Regal T-Bird. And then what beat what. If a pair of Superformances beat three FFRs or the other way around. If a Diva beat a Gull Wing. How many Speedsters it took to beat a straight of Cobras. If Lambos should be wild. Did a Shoebox Ford trump everything. What should we call a royal flush. "Please don't use that word," I said. "Sorry," she said. "I forgot." Finally it just got crazy. We spent the rest of Friday watching judge shows, Mathis, Joe Brown, Judy, people incapable of being embarrassed suing each other over cell phone bills and pit bull bites, twiddling our thumbs.

Saturday came on sunny. We entertained the thought of salvaging a day run out to Carlisle. But my innards were still too storm-wracked to leave the house. This time we decided to make ourselves useful. A few days earlier I'd finished a major section of the novel. Got my kid to the milestone age of nineteen. Brought the page count up to 835. We took the morning to look at how much of the story still remained. Last year, in April, I used this column to describe how I'd written the thing so far in patches, scenes like auto parts, no attention to structure or assembly. The effort since then had gone toward putting things together. I hauled out all the stuff I still had left. Maybe 500 pages of unassembled scenes. Toni suggested using the still-empty stalls of the flea market on the family room floor to lay them all out.

We spent most of the day going through them. Neither of us admitted to the darkening atmosphere of dread at all the work still on the floor. I was shot. I'd stolen so much time from the business it had gone to hell. My friends were memories. My kids were strangers. What stood there, up and down the aisles of the flea market, was as much as another year of this, with no stamina, no wherewithal to keep going. Late that afternoon, while things down at Carlisle were breaking up for the day, Toni reached a breakthrough. "You know what?" she said. I didn't. "You're done," she said. Yeah, I said, I know. "No," she said. "I mean your novel."

Change the venue to your garage. Around you the floor is littered with unused parts, fenders, brake assemblies, hoses, bags of bolts, seats, bumpers, gauges, hoods, a tranny, taillight assemblies, radiators. "No," you say. "I've still got all this stuff to go." You get this gentle forbearing look you've used yourself on old relatives at varying stages of Alzheimer's. You realize your mouth is open and nothing you do will close it. "All this stuff," says Toni, "it's a second book. The first one's done." Your head reels. Birds lift off the desert the concept is so out of nowhere. "Look at what you've got," she says. "It's done." Sure enough. There it was, 835 pages, seven parts, 88 chapters, 350 thousand words, a kid from the age of twelve to nineteen, at the airport now, in a new suit, leaving home, knowing what lies behind him but not, where he's going, what lies ahead. Sometimes you can't see what you've done for what you haven't. She was right. Up from all the knee-deep rubble of everything you think you've still got left stands a finished car. Not what you thought it would be. But all it needs is polish. Here's the key. Fire it up. Go out and get a life again.

No Requiem

It came back in March. An e-mail from Dave the President announcing the decision by the officers to kill the New Jersey Replicar Club. The kill site would be a restaurant, close to where we used to meet in the break room of Warren's kitchen and bath business, and the funeral service a dinner, scheduled for April. Food was on the club, funded out of the treasury, and whatever we didn't burn would go to charity. Drinks were dutch.

It was a tough e-mail. I tend to take for granted that institutions as important in my life as the NJRC will always be there no matter what I wander off and do. That there will always be good people tending to their perpetuation. Dave's e-mail was like hearing that they were converting my high school to a tanning salon, dissolving the Army, selling the New York Mets to Fresno. But when I looked at my own slow disengagement over the last three years I wasn't surprised. Things had been petering out. Not because we didn't have great officers. For the second season in a row, Dave and John and the rest of the team had hammered out an itinerary of events, action stuff like racing sessions at Pocono, gymkhanas, auto mechanics lessons at Wade's, rallies, that nobody much paid attention to. For a year and a half, John had doggedly patched together and mailed out one great newsletter after another, despite the fact that there wasn't much to write about and his audience had left the building. He'd also maintained a website that saw so little traffic it got to be like mowing grass around the headstones in the yard of a crumbling Moravian church.

It goes without saying that it wasn't always like this. The club was founded in January 1991 by Tim Lewis and four independent and idiosyncratic guys with long-held dreams in their heads and scary crates in their garages. For most of its first decade, it was a builder's club, guys helping guys put cars together. By 2000, when I came along, the NJRC was robust and flourishing, and even had the redeeming social value that wives and girlfriends somehow bestow on the worst of guy things. There were years when the membership routinely topped a hundred. Big rowdy monthly meetings. Seasons packed with events, from early spring shakedown drives to blow the mouse nests out of the mufflers, to Carlisle, to Memorial Motor Madness in the parking lot of the M&M factory, to the Shawnee and Solberg Balloon Festivals, to the Chocolate Festival, to the Tri-State VW Show, to the Southern Adventure, to the Blues and Wine and Retro Weekends at Waterloo Village, to the Annual NJRC Summer Picnic where Bobbi would bring her famous ambrosia, Warren his secret barbecue sauce, Linda and Rocky the sweetest and tenderest corn, where you could sit back in your lawn chair with a Rolling Rock and openly admire women in bathing suits while they climbed sparkling out of the water of a pool or lake. Every season ended in October with the Popcorn Rally, following John's meticulous maps of two-lane roads through fifty miles of breathtaking country and achingly beautiful late autumn foliage, answering Rocky's inscrutable riddles along the way, arguing with him about the answers afterward. Gray? But there wasn't a dog next to that pond, Rocky. Well, there was three days ago, and gray's the right answer. Peppered through these mainstay events was the spontaneous stuff, the cruise nights, impromptu runs up to Hawk's Nest, Tommy's welding workshops, charity shows, parades where the Cobras would chase the kids off the curbs to get to streetside shade where they could briefly cool their simmering engines down. Around Superbowl time, to combat RDD, we'd gather for an annual banquet at venues like the Butler VFW Hall, where we held our annual Gumball Challenge, a pinewood derby race on a track it was Larry's job to haul around. There were guys like Jerry who made the two-plus-hour drive from Long Island, running the gauntlet of Queens and Manhattan, to hang with us. Mark and Sandy and Frank who spent almost that much road time from deep down the Jersey shore. Alan and Rocky from Pennsylvania. In its heyday the draw of the NJRC reached across the Northeast and down the seaboard as far as Florida.

When did it begin to end? When did we reach "peak club" and start down the other side? Cobra guys don't think like Speedster guys, MG guys don't think like GT40 guys, Jaguar guys don't think like Mercedes guys, Grand Sport guys don't think like Ferrari or Allard guys, and you never know what Diva guys are thinking, so the post mortems have as much contentious diversity as our cars. You'll hear it was when our meetings leaned too hard into bureaucratic stuff like incorporation and insurance. When we had the Great Logo Battle. When guys and gals who'd weathered ten to fifteen years of rain in cars waterproofed with duct tape started using their daily drivers to get to Carlisle instead. Truth is, nobody can nail that tipping point, because it isn't there. It just sneaked in underneath us, slow and inexorable as floodwater, and then kept happening. Folks move on. Some move away. Summer weekends get choked with soccer matches and grandkids. Harry takes Renata and retires. Tim hooks up with Doug Foley to run a top fuel dragster in the IHRA. Paul, after serving as President and Door Kicker, starts playing guitar in his church band, and Wednesday is rehearsal night. Warren sells his business and our clubhouse goes with it. Andy, after two Cobras and a Speedster, gets deep into the whole revival of the doodlebug. Bill, after blowing two engines at Louden and racing his Daytona at the Glen, gets into living on a yacht. Other guys sell their cars for engagement rings, medical bills, nursery furniture, divorce settlements. Nobody at fault.

But how do you kill a club? Start shooting? Throw your membership cards in a fire barrel and do some weird nude dance around it? Push all your cars off the Palisades into the Hudson? Hire a suicide bomber, form a circle, join hands? Pick each other's bones in a restaurant? Back on that afternoon in April, when Toni and I got to the kill site, there everybody was, except for those who sadly couldn't make it, and it wasn't long before Tommy and Rocky and Phil and me and a couple of other guys were in the bar, buying each other drinks, catching up to where Tommy got to telling his pipefitter jokes, Rocky the story about using his shoelaces when his accelerator cable broke, plenty of car talk, all the touchstones there the way they are with brothers. How do you kill this? You don't. You retire the mold and acknowledge the work that held you together long enough to form a family. Give what's left in the treasury to Ronald McDonald House. Put the rest of the NJRC machinery and its historic run of almost eighteen years on blocks for now. No kill. No requiem. Just gratitude — deep and enduring — for friends you'll have for life.

The Car Whisperer

There are cars in this hobby that never see the light of SEMA, Speed Channel, Knott's and the Carlisle Nationals, even the hometown neon of a drive-in cruise night. They typically share the same genesis. A guy buys a kit or roller with the vision of building the dream ride of his childhood. Then one of a thousand things happens. He learns that a full-size roadable car can't be put together with Testor's cement and a bicycle wrench. Or, more heart than aptitude, he gets to where he's reached this Rube Goldberg point he can't begin to reverse engineer his way back from. Or he takes it all the way through, drives it long enough to put the dream to rest, then moves on. A hurricane, kids, illness, death, another reserve unit deployment, fire, the economic collapse of the country, there are a thousand possible paths that all lead to the same destination. A car that started as a pure and irrepressible vision and then got left to atrophy and moulder, increasingly buried under the rubble a shed or garage was invented to collect, its heart leaking air, its spirit going to sludge in its oil pan, its soul turning to varnish in its float bowls. Enter the Car Whisperer. A guy named Alan Merklin.

Alan has renovated and rodded cars since high school when he was cutting his reading teeth on *Mechanix Illustrated* and Hank Felsen novels like *Hot Rod* and *Boy Gets Car*. Sometime after he graduated, he hooked up with Larry Middleton, the owner of Four Cylinder Motors in the Jersey burb of Hackettstown. The two of them became buddies and worked out a timeshare deal where Alan used Larry's shop to rehabilitate old daily drivers, run them to MAACO for the quick wrap of a paint job, and sell them off the strip of asphalt out in front of Larry's shop on Route 46. Strictly free-lance, part time, as supplemental income to his day gig as a trucker to support his growing family, Alan managed to reclaim and sell in the neighborhood of 30 to 40 cars a year off that strip, making sure that Jersey's vital workforce of minimum-wage employees had af-fordable and reliable and briefly fancy transportation.

Then, some twenty years ago, he spotted a derelict Bradley GTII in a garage in another Jersey town. He'd always been drawn to ex-otic-looking cars. Back then, in the *Mechanix Illustrated* kind of way he was familiar with, the Bradley was as exotic as it got. He bought it off the TWA pilot who owned it. It had no brakes, door gaps he could pass the Jersey phone book through, gas in the tank so old he could have bottled it as Johnny Walker Blue. In short order, he cleaned its tank, got its brakes back, did what he could for its doors, revitalized its mechanical and electrical legs, got its Type I engine working, detailed everything, stuck a sign in its window, and parked it out on Route 46. In less than an hour it was gone. He'd made a minor profit. He was hooked.

Thus began his pursuit to rescue "disappeared" kit cars and hot rods. At first, he relied on his friends, his truck routes, his fellow truckers to find them. He started hitting the Carlisle Nationals. He joined the New Jersey Replicar Club. Soon he was pulling Bradleys, Gazelles, MGTDs, and other defeated projects out of the burial sites of garages and sheds across the Northeast, giving them a second run at life in the hands of new owners. Somewhere in there his marriage ended. He took a Fonzie apartment above a garage and kept going. The Internet happened. He met a Pennsylvania gal named Kim through an on-line personal ad. At the time he was reconstituting a red Ziata. When he first drove out to Chambersburg for an in-person introduction, in the red Ziata he was working on, Kim fell in love with it and made him leave it there. He had to borrow her car to get back home to Jersey. Within a year, after a courtship that saw the Ziata make 38 interstate trips, they were married and living in Chambersburg. Alan started using Ebay Motors to find strays to put back into circulation. Until now, shallow on discretionary cash but deep on a reservoir of streetwise exuberance, he'd relied pretty much on the borrowed trailer, the rented U-Haul, the bartered use of somebody's shop or welding rig, rough-and-tumble karma, on whatever wit and improvisation it took to do the job. In Chambersburg he settled in. Bought a trailer. Had the local Amish build him a shop barn. Assembled a quality local network of paint shop, upholsterer, and master machinist capable of fabricating any part the car of the moment needed. Kim would go along with him in the cab of his little Chevy pickup on his interstate search-and-rescues. He'd find them in dirt, on sawhorses, tacked together with drywall screws, hurt in other unspeakable ways, and bring them home, coax them back, get personal with them to where he'd tell us, earnest as a missionary, that he was keeping them. And then, just as he got to where he had us, turn every one of them around. Nashville, we'd hear. Kenosha. Seattle.

A couple of nights ago I gave him a call to get an inventory of his rescues. He was at the Great Frederick County Fair in Maryland, with Kim, waiting for Kelly Pickler to take the stage. They found a bench, sat down, put a list together. He ranks his projects in three ways. Resales are those that need to be tuned, re-hosed, re-belted, re-braked, painted, surface mechanical and electrical and cosmetic stuff to bring back their looks and reliability. Rehabs are what the rest of us could call lost causes. Builds, of course, are his out-of-the crate jobs. In all, he and Kim remembered seventeen resales, sixteen rehabs, and twelve builds, encompassing Bradleys, Gazelles, MGTDs, 53 Corvettes, Marlenes, Shays, 27 Ford Roadsters, Ziatas, and 23 T-buckets. A Trimuter electric three-wheeler and a Thunder Ranch Riot are in there. The last few years he's settled on Speedsters, four of them resales, six rehabs, five of them builds, from classic to outlaw to street rod versions. Close to fifty cars, rescued from all across the country, delivered to owners from Florida to Washington, California to Vermont, Texas to Wisconsin, Colorado to Connecticut, Illinois and Indiana to Kentucky and Georgia and Alabama, and most states in between. His recaptured beauties see cruise nights. They get featured. They earn trophies. They drive the foreign roads of Holland, Belgium, Germany, and the United Arab Emirates. He's still a trucker, recently an indie, freelancing as a car hauler, but he's been thinking lately of relinquishing what he still calls just a hobby. Currently he's down to a triple-black Vintage Speedster, a car he loves for its solid and simple honesty, and a crotchrocket-powered homebuilt go-kart capable of 130 mph. Keepers this time? Sure, Alan. Like I keep beer. You're not gonna quit until the day the sun don't set on a saved-by-Merklin reclamation.

So don't tell us you're getting tired. Just tell us what it is you whisper.

2009

Under the Floor

In the concrete floor of my garage, in the back corner where I keep my Speedster, there's a trap door, a two-foot square of concrete with a flush-mounted handle, an inset lock, sturdy hinges, cased in a steel rim like the hole where it seats in the floor. I've never had the key. I've never drilled the lock out. All I've done is verify that nothing vital to the house — furnace, water heater, oil tank, fuse box, septic tank, leach field — is hidden underneath it. My sons have hounded me for years about opening it. I've never said no. All I've said is that I'd think about it.

And I have. For sixteen years. Where it could lead. Here's what I have to work with. We live on top of a ridge with a house close in on either side of ours. Young families with little kids. Out back, the ridge falls away in a steep hillside of rock, maybe a hundred feet to where it levels out for forty feet of woods before butting up against the yards of the houses below us. In front, there's a rise up to the road, and the houses of neighbors on the other side. Not much reason to dig a hideout or tunnel. If we had an old abbey next door, or a skinhead compound, or a nudist colony, it'd be easy. The way it is, wherever that door leads, it would have to go for maybe seven miles to come up under something even remotely worth it.

Back in the seventies I bought a Speedster off a college kid from one of Salt Lake's wealthier neighborhoods who was studying philosophy. It was a rustbucket, held together with bondo and the tensile strength of maybe eight different paint jobs, a top with half the stitching rotted out, an engine that had lost one cylinder and was barely hanging on to its last three. But there it was. The indestructible force of that ageless shape. He was asking twelve hundred. I offered him four. A college kid myself, an engineering student with a young wife, it was all I had. When he got done screaming, and told me some girl who wanted it was waiting to get a loan approved, I showed him my four hundred cash and told him to keep me in mind. Three weeks later he called. The girl hadn't got her loan. In the meantime, the Speedster's tranny had exploded, the rebuild had cost him four hundred, and all he wanted now was the cost of the rebuild back. A friend drove me out to get it after work. I handed the kid the cash, got in my new Speedster, and was firing it up when his mother appeared in the passenger window, all screeching rage and teeth, calling me a thief and crook and hoodlum for taking advantage of her son. She chased me down the street, still screeching through the window, until the engine found enough momentum to handle second gear and leave her standing in the cracked haze of the mirror.

My niece the Harry Potter fan probably has the most fun imagining what's down beneath my locked trap door. My nephew keeps a real-life Halo World there. My sons and I have this vast garage filled with every car we've ever wanted. Toni has herself a tropical island with the world's biggest karaoke system and an endless line of waiters in Speedos bringing her Cosmopolitans on the beach. My neighbor John thinks we've got Dick Cheney down there. Aside from my old GTO and a hundred other wish wheels, the stuff I keep on the other side of that door includes a club where I play jazz trumpet, a Pulitzer Prize, and my favorite landscape — the reservation country of southern Utah and northern Arizona where I grew up.

That afternoon, limping on failing cylinders, spongy with rust, me in the busted driver's seat, grinning through the cracked windshield like the happy thief I'd inadvertently become, I brought the Speedster home. I'd been married a year and a half to an absolute dream of a girl, beautiful and loving, blond hair, this bottomless reservoir of unqualified kindness. I built mobile homes and went to night school. She worked as a surgical assistant in a children's hospital. In my dirty teeshirt I invited her for a ride. She still had her hospital smell. She looked troubled in a way I'd never seen her look. I'd seen her hurt. This wasn't that. This was something intuitive, foreboding, like I'd introduced some turning point into our marriage that she alone could sense the distance of. We headed out. At some point, looking down into her footwell, she asked me what was under the piece of particle board on the floor beneath her sandals. Lift it up, I told her, take a look. She did. And then nothing. I looked over and saw that she was crying. Not out loud. Just her face wet where she was looking through the windshield and the wind blew her hair aside. I looked down into her footwell. There was a ragged hole there big enough to fall through, and this moving smear of asphalt that was the street, a street named South Temple because it originated on the south side of Temple Square, home to the forbidding granite building in one of whose secret rooms we'd been married a year and a half ago.

I didn't know what moved her to cry. All I saw was street. But sure enough. Within two years I had the Speedster in shape, a floor pan of thick steel and a powerful engine, and was out racing it. Within another two years I was done with engineering school. Within another year, done with racing, sleepless, this night highway of ghost trucks roaring through my head, I was taking the Speedster out at one or two in the morning, the stinger bolted on to drown out the roar of the trucks, pounding up and down the canyons of the Wasatch Front until my head was clear enough to drive down 80 back into the city, pretending I'd never been here and was only passing through. Before long I was done with everything else. A degree I'd been told I needed in order to be responsible. An unforgiving upbringing in a take-no-prisoners religion. A place I'd come unhinged in. Kindness. We sold the Speedster and most everything else we owned. She moved to Portland because she liked rain. I moved east.

It wasn't the Speedster. It sure wasn't her. It didn't take long in the east to discover how lucky and stupid and cruel I'd been. But it took years to get that undeservingly lucky again. Now, at the end of a long day, I take my second Speedster out to get lost in the miles of hills and farmland here in northwest Jersey, and come home knowing this is where I'm from. In the garage, idling the Speedster back into place over the locked trap door, there's still the reflex to contemplate what lies on the other side. A patch of moving asphalt just through the hole. A street like a river running just inches underneath my house and what I've learned how to love.

Convertibles with Heads

There's this movie in my head that starts like this. A desert village somewhere south of Hermosillo. A couple of chickens peck the seeds out of sheep droppings scattered across the dirt yard of a shipping crate of a house. In the middle of the yard, a woman dressed in black works a manual sewing machine, her dusty feet rocking the treadle while her hands guide this bright yellow cloth under the reciprocating needle. Out in the road, two kids are filling a blue plastic bucket with sand, while a large red cow with a sleeping man on its back looks for grass around the roots of sunflowers. Across the yard is a tin-roofed building that used to be a stable. Inside, skilled artisans, plying a trade they learned from their uncles, lay sheets of woven fiberglass across a mold formed by the carefully arranged bodies of six dozing women, then paint the sheets with honey-colored resin. You can start to see, as hips give way to fenders, where this is going. Flies chase the slow blades of a ventilator fan turning in the daylight of an open circle in the roof. One end of the large room, in shadow, holds a collection of maybe forty electric guitars, hazed white with dust.

My buddy Rocky hasn't been right since the time I hit him in the head. Four summers ago, heading for Hawk's Nest one Saturday afternoon in our Speedsters, just a couple of convertibles with heads, he was riding behind me when one of my tires caught a rock, sent it airborne, and put it where he drove right into it. The thing skimmed the top of his windshield frame and smacked him in the forehead. I've told him a thousand times to lower his seats and get the top half of his head down where his windshield can protect it. Aside from being flat out dangerous, it's embarrassing to walk into a biker bar or ice cream stand with a happy-looking guy who's got his head flecked with bug juice from the eyebrows up. I didn't know I'd hit him until we'd run Hawk's Nest a couple of times, a roller-coaster little twisted piece of road that hangs off the side of a cliff above the Delaware River. We'd stopped at an overlook before making another couple of runs and then heading down the far side of the mountain for beers at the bar where the road meets the river again. Straight down, way down below us, on the river, the rafters and the inner tubers weren't much more than specks. That was when he told me about the rock. I looked. Sure enough, in there with the bug juice, I could see the red bruise, the bump, the scratches. And there was something in his eyes, something new, a peaceful look, like every day of the rest of his life was going to be Christmas.

The movie that runs in my head only runs, like now, in winter, in the heart of January, the time of year when I can no longer remember or even imagine going outside in just a teeshirt, driving with the windows open or the top down, or why cars and houses come with air conditioning. Internet groups take on the solicitous attitude of suicide prevention hotlines. Guys with astonishing faith in the laws of the solar system start planning for Carlisle. Out behind the converted stable where they make bodies for various replicas, depending on how the women are arranged, a yellow horse with a rope halter stands dozing in a slice of shade. The shells of Cobras and Divas and Speedsters cure in the sunlight of a dirt lot. Cargo containers are scattered around like derailed boxcars. Hand-lettered signs tell you what components they hold. Tarps are draped over stacks of tires. Farther on, three women wearing shawls are working small boards back and forth along the flanks and fenders of a Cobra. Still farther on, in an outdoor shop staked off with sagging chain link nailed to posts, a diesel engine drives a generator for two hooded welders cutting pieces of tubing into a frame. Out across the desert, dirt rises like a waking snake out of a low range of mountains, chasing the howl of a wound-out lunatic V-8.

Hawk's Nest is a popular hang most every summer weekend. Meaning that traffic can be pretty thick when you make the long climb out of Port Jervis up the mountain to where the real ride starts, where the whole left side of the world falls away, where the road is mostly a crooked ramshackle shelf of asphalt and stone tacked by mortar to a cliff hundreds of feet above the Delaware. Rocky has a neat trick for making it a good ride. Just before we get to the crest, he slows way down, starts hanging back, letting the traffic in front pull way ahead. By the time we get to the good stuff we're looking at a clean half mile of one of the wildest little stretches of paving on the planet. Hammer down. A wall of rock on one side. Nothing but sky on the other, sky and a shallow stone wall and a couple of overlooks, the overlooks crowded with bikes and the chicks who ride their back fenders. You could see them waving if you looked. But you don't. All you care about is keeping up with the back of Rocky's head, getting through there fast, because everything in your life that you've never slowed down enough to be forgiven for is right behind you.

My friend John has been tinkering with his Diva as long as I've known him. Different engines, gearing, suspension setups, you name it. The evolution of both machine and man was directionless at first. And then one summer afternoon he ran Hawk's Nest with us. It was his first run. Rocky in front, me next, John in back, we hammered through there, outrunning every dog we'd ever thought of kicking, and then tore down the sweeping switchbacks off the far side of the mountain. I could see John's head smoke in my rear view mirror. I could smell the delirious fear of his hair on fire. It was the day his tinkering found a destiny. Full race. Now, two years later, the Diva is a wicked thing, malevolent dark green and black, tricked out with racing slicks, racing seat, HANS device, the works. He runs Pocono on their road course days. He talks racing the same wild-eyed zealous way joggers talk running: to where you want to crack him in the forehead with a rock.

I take my welding helmet off. Rocky comes out of the stable, cracking a Coke, his dust mask perched on his head like a birthday hat. We stand there, watching the Diva break the last hill, hit the desert floor, come howling our way, the black seed of a massive cloud of raging dirt. In my personal suicide prevention movie, the movie I run all winter to keep from hurting myself until we're out running for real again, it's time for a couple of tacos and some refried beans.

Distance Traveled

We were Utah teenagers, my buddies and me, back when they were building Interstate 80 across Nevada. I remember them doing it in long patches. Every time you came across one of the desert towns — Elko, Battle Mountain, Winnemucca — the slab of the freeway would end in a long dike of graded dirt, and barriers would shunt you off into town, onto the main drag, where all the mom and pop casinos were. At the end, past the last light, a road would shunt you back out to another long patch of 80. It seemed to be like that for years. We figured, back then, that Nevada had made a law to keep herding tourists through its desert towns, to keep its towns from going broke, and that 80 across Nevada would always be like this. We'd stop for gas is all. Make sure the pump jockey didn't squirt oil on the alternator. Heading out of Salt Lake, crossing the Salt Flats to Wendover where Nevada started, we had Reno to get to, or Tahoe, once San Jose, where one of us knew this girl who had friends for the rest of us. We'd go just on possibility, heads blasted by sun and wind in the open windows of a 57 Pontiac, a 59 Impala, a supercharged 40 Ford, even a 58 Rambler that snapped an axle once on the way out of Lovelock.

On a beach in the Dominican Republic, where Toni and I spent a week barefoot and in a state of relaxed inebriation in the company of the Car Whisperer and his wife Kim back in February, Alan and I would talk the easy days away the way car guys do, with stories from when we were younger that had to do with driving, raising hell, looking to score. Since he's a Jersey boy, he had the crazier stories, and his rites of passage came much earlier than mine. But on the last afternoon we stumbled onto the topic of distance traveled for a girl. Being from out west, where hundreds of miles separate one possibility from the next, I had it all over him. Salt Lake to Portland, almost 800 miles up through Idaho, across the Blue Mountains, then west along the Columbia. Later on, south to Tucson, another 800 miles, down Highway 89 across the high red desolate country between Kanab and Page, then down through Phoenix. Still later, north to Missoula, over 500 miles up along the backside of the Tetons. Alan drives interstates for a living. I wasn't counting on impressing him.

"This something you did often?" he asks.

"Regularly."

From our chaises in the shade, we watch a fiftyish woman come walking up out of the water, her bikini top in her hand, everything tanned the color of wet leather.

"Why?" he said. "Salt Lake didn't have any girls?"

"They all had missionaries they were waiting for."

"I never had to leave Jersey. Until Kim."

"When you got it right."

"Yep. Okay."

The San Jose girls materialized, took one hostile look at us, four leering Utah hayseeds with the wrong car, the wrong hair, the wrong clothes, the totally wrong bucktoothed expectations, yokels who'd hee-hawed their way across Nevada like a quartet of midnight cowboys, and turned to smoke as quick as they'd materialized. I remember the sting of their giggling contempt as they turned away and walked out of the reach of possibility. Years later, of course, 80 was made continuous across Nevada, and the desert towns used business loops and forty-story signs to lure the big spenders off the freeway. By then we'd also learned, probably from watching West Side Story, to play it cool, not to leer like coyotes in the presence of romantic possibility, and were getting places with girls. Sure Salt Lake had them. No reason to leave. But for me there was always this sense of road and destination in the mix. A girl waiting somewhere. Opening her door to see me on her porch like somehow I'd come home. Like somehow I'd earned whatever she felt like giving me beyond a porch hug. "I just put some Cream of Mushroom on. You look like you could use some."

Alan got up to get another mojito. I was remembering the twisted switchbacks and runaway lanes coming off the Blue Mountains into Pendleton. The headwinds across the Oregon plateau that skated my old Catalina around like I'd never aligned it. The cutting airborne dirt when I stopped at a highway burger joint. The sign on the sprung glass door that read, "Yes. The wind always blows. Don't ask." The hard-eyed little blonde at the counter who looked outside at my derelict car and then at me like she was daring me to ask her. The deer I clipped coming south one night through Montana with incense in my nose. The night I went through Phoenix and smelled, in the freeway exhaust, the sudden scent of fresh orange. I was remembering the Missoula girl, the Tucson girl, my young ex-wife in Portland before either of us yet understood that what had driven us apart was permanent. I was remembering the exotic road cars I always imagined I was driving. And then, two chaises away, yukking it up with Kim, I was remembering Toni, and the drive I made that eventually led me to her. The first night across Wyoming. The funeral procession across heavily patrolled Nebraska. Iowa, Illinois, Indiana, Ohio. Forty nonstop hours except for gas and food and coffee. By Pennsylvania I was hallucinating. The heads of my friends were taking turns appearing on the hood. Just shy of the George Washington Bridge, where a sign announced the end of 80, I realized I'd driven all of it, in patches, coast to coast. When Alan got back I was ready.

"2200 miles," I said. "Salt Lake to New York. Straight."

"For a girl?"

"Eventually."

"Okay," he says. "You got me."

It was getting toward sunset. Bikini tops were going on and leaving. On the other side of Alan, past his mojito, after a barefoot week of unleashed exuberance and sparkling laughter, Toni and Kim were quiet, mourning the end of the best vacation I've ever had, contemplating staying there. "We could always fold towels," Kim said. "I'd do that." We took our last walk down to the almost deserted beach and said goodbye.

At Carlisle, if you see me looking too long at a GT40, Ultima, GTM, Diablo, 904, or another dream of a road car, don't worry. I'm just out for a ride. Chasing the ribbon of 89 between Kanab and Page. Sailing up through Idaho. Blasting across Nevada. Snaking down the switchbacks off the Blues, hitting the plateau, stopping at a windswept burger joint with a sign on the door, a little blonde at the counter with an attitude I remember from San Jose. "Excuse me for asking," I say, "but does it always blow like this?" She looks outside. Sees what I'm driving this time. Her eyes go big and soft. "Sure does, mister. Ask all you want."

The Magic Hat

It finally happens. Where Bruce Meyers, the heart and soul and spirit of the dune buggy, is the Carlisle Featured Guest, and Johnny "Hoss" Hallstrand offers to let me wear his big ten-gallon hat. I'm blown away. He tells me it's magic. Suddenly I'm nervous. "If it's magic," I ask him, "how come it let Dan Blocker die?" "It's not that magic," he says, "but it makes some neat stuff happen."

We're surrounded by the usual Carlisle Yahoos. Among the standouts is Jim Ignacio, aka MusbJim, who's flown from California wearing one of those FlairHair Visor things, a full head of black porcupine hair tinged with pale orange fire, on a dare to get the TSA to waterboard him. Lunatic people who've taken more lethal risks than wearing a magic hat. Hoss, who had the chops to drive his Subie-powered Cabriolet from Tennessee, takes it off. I take and put it on.

"How does it work?" I ask. Hoss shrugs. "It just does." "What do you do?" I ask him. We wait while an engine winds up on the dyno truck, howls for a couple of seconds, then dies in this clatter of a million liberated pieces. We look. Up on the rack a gutshot Peugeot is smoking like a rained-out bonfire. "Think clean thoughts," says Hoss.

And so, under the usual fickle Carlisle overcast, thinking of angels singing my father's favorite hymn, I take Toni and strike out to see what Carlisle 2009 has to offer. With a bad limp, from a knee I blew out in March helping a friend lift his Speedster body off its busted chassis onto a new one, I'm closer to Festus than I am to Hoss. We do the MGs, the Triumphs, the Volvos, the Audis, the Japanese sports jobs. We do the dune buggies, the Cobras, the Lambos, the Ferraris, the GT40s, the Valkyries, the Lotus Seven knockoffs. People fold up their lawn chairs and leave when they see us coming. Toni wonders if she should be wearing an Indian feather and beaded headband. We do the Car Corral and the Building Z Food Court. People dump their egg sandwiches and leave when they see us coming. We do a stroll through Building Y. Then we head for Building T to take in the manufacturers.

The place has been evacuated. The cars are there, and the displays, but not the people. "Fire drill?" says Toni. "Could be swine flu," I tell her. "Don't touch anything." Which is a shame, because every Cobra, Thunderbird, GT40, Speedster, Lambo, Daytona, and hot rod in the place has a sign in its windshield that says "Free," even Factory Five's new Roadster, and as we wander past them mystified, every ignition switch has a key in it. We head for the KCB booth to ask Boss Jim what's going on. It's empty too. Just a handwritten sign that says free subscriptions. There's a note addressed to us from QueenBee. It tells us to come to Building X. "There isn't a Building X," says Toni. "There's Y and T and Z. No X." "Well," I say, "there's directions to it."

We follow them outside, through the maze of the abandoned

Flea Market, to a cinderblock bunker the size of a National Park outhouse. Sure enough. A sign says Building X. We go inside. Just a lobby with an escalator down. "There's no up escalator," Toni says. "Maybe it's got a reverse," I say. "Let's find out."

So we get on. It takes us down the white-tiled maw of a long shaft. Soon we've lost sight of the entrance. Without the amber coach lamps embedded every few feet in the tile walls we'd be riding blind. I've never seen an escalator that can turn corners, like a cave or a creek, as it descends. Toni tightens her grip on my arm. I hold onto Hoss's hat. The wind up the shaft turns cold and heavy. I start to imagine things. The cries of night animals. The tombs of a Transylvanian cathedral. The scurry of rats with the faces of dead saints. It goes forever. And then I can start to smell salt, feel the air start to get more buoyant, the wind turn balmier, blood circulate in my arm as Toni starts to relax. Below us the amber lights start giving way to the kind of light and shadow only sunlight makes. The shaft pulls back. I look down at the tops of palm trees. Sand between them. Music. A song I recognize about a 409. A beach and then the rise and crash of ocean waves and surfboards going airborne. Dune buggies everywhere. The escalator brings us down through palm fronds. Toni grabs a coconut. She's wearing a pink bikini now. I'm in a grass skirt. We step off the escalator barefoot.

Everyone's there. The Cobra guys are barbecuing steaks the size of Massachusetts. The Citroen guys are doing snails on a hibachi. The Speedster guys have chili and bananas going. "Look!" says Toni. "The Beach Boys!" We spot Harold Pace up in a palm tree lobbing coconuts down at a Volvo guy with a white nose. QueenBee and her sister Judi taking a hula class from a big Samoan-looking guy. Steve Temple wandering among the blankets with a tube of Coppertone asking chicks if they'd like their backs greased up. Alan the Car Whisperer talking consolingly into the stinger pipe of a sad-looking dune buggy. "Where's Kim?" Toni asks him. "Folding towels," he says. "She got a job. She ain't leaving." Out on the beach, where the waves run themselves out, Bruce Meyers and John Denmat are screaming back and forth in the new Manx Kick-Out SS they just put the final touches on, kicking up four rooster tails of foam and sand. We find Boss Jim in a beach chaise. I'm glad to see he's in a grass skirt too. "Nice hat," he says, getting up, swapping his mojito to his left hand so we can shake. "It's borrowed," I say. "I need to give it back." I've never seen Boss Jim move faster. He grabs my arm just as I go take the hat off. The Beach Boys stop cold in the second verse of Little Deuce Coupe. Bruce and John bring the Manx to a skidding sidelong halt. The place draws a collective gasp. All you can hear is the waves and the sizzle of snail juice. Everyone's looking. "Don't you touch that hat," Boss Jim says.

And so I keep it on. Through the afternoon. The sunset. The bonfire we gather around. Lane Anderson sings Venus in his velvet Charleston voice. A Citroen guy sings La Marseillaise. I sing my father's favorite hymn. In the glow of the dying fire, with long snaking lines of moonlight off the quiet waves, Bruce Meyers strums his six-string, tells us stories from his storied past, and says it's time to finally go. Everyone looks my way. "Noooo!" I hear Kim scream from the towel room. "I'm not done!" "Sorry," I tell them. "Not yet." MusbJim steps up, his FlairHair tipped with silver in the moonlight, and puts his arm around my shoulder. "We'll do it together," he says. "My hair. Your hat. On three."

A Car Called Wait

The day starts off, like it has since March, with rain. And the news that Jim Ignacio, MusbJim, the Flair Hair Visor guy who rescued me from under the magic bong of Hoss Hallstrand's hat in Carlisle back in May, just turned a hundred thousand kilometers on his odometer. I'm curious what mine says. In the garage I quietly snap the dusty tonneau on the Speedster back to take a look. It's already awake. I hope it hasn't heard the news about Jim.

Let's get outta here, it says. Come on. I'm dying.

It's raining, I say. You hate rain.

Only time I see you, it says, is when you come out here to take the freakin' Audi somewhere. Or dump the garbage. Or sneak a smoke in winter.

I can't help the rain, I say. I wish I could.

Outside the closed garage where we're having this conversation, it's coming down, on the driveway, on the roof, down through the leaves of the big oaks, the way it has since March when it got warm enough for weather to be liquid. The deck off the back has been pressure washed but can't dry out enough to take a coat of stain. Down off the deck the yard is a satellite view of the Amazon. The Speedster hasn't seen sunlight since October. Crippled by a bad miss it picked up last year, flatlined by a drained battery, shackled by a procrastinating owner who can't get up the will to even knock the dust off, it sits here, in its back corner of the garage, surrounded by accumulated cardboard I haven't packed up and carted to the recycling place since Christmas. And it wants to know what we're still doing in New Jersey.

We live here, I say. For now, anyway.

You hear about Jim Ignacio?

Yeah, I say.

His Speedster just turned a hundred thousand, it says.

Kilometers, I say. Baby miles. They don't mean anything.

They mean sixty-three thousand miles, it says. Real ones.

Yeah, I say. Sixty-three thousand easy year-round southern California miles.

They're still miles, it says.

Is that what you want? Have me wear you out? Make you old before your time?

It beats sitting here getting arthritis, it says. Staring at sheet rock.

I can put a poster up for now. A nice road one.

A poster, it says. Listen to yourself.

Look, I say. I'm in a slump. I'm in a bad way.

I want to go back to California, it says. Hawaiian Gardens. I never should have left.

You were in pieces back then, I say. A basket case. Tell me one thing you remember about California.

Sixty-three thousand miles, it says. What am I up to? Maybe ten?

I know it can't see its odometer any more than I can look inside my ear.

You're getting close to forty, I say, thinking so this is what it feels like, lying to a car.

It doesn't feel like forty, it says. Unless you mean dog miles.

Look, I say. Next week. I'll take a whole day off. Fix you up. Take you out.

I want Danny back, it says. He's cool. He knows what he's doing. He takes care of business.

Danny Piperato, I'm thinking, my buddy from upstate New York, who drove his Spyder down one Saturday last summer to work on fixing the engine miss, and left me with finish-up instructions I've never followed. I'm not sure he'd want to waste his time again.

I can handle it, I say. I just gotta wait to get your hinges back from Alan.

I can run without a stupid deck lid, it says. You ran your old one that way.

Toni wouldn't be seen in you without a deck lid, I say.

So leave her here, it says. Like we used to.

Careful, I say. She's the only reason you're not a primered rat rod. The only reason you got a real paint job. And carpet.

Sorry, it says.

Me too, I say. I'd like to get out too. Believe me. Don't forget the good times.

The least you could do, it says, is finally name me.

That's easy, I say. What kind of name do you want?

Something like Dave's Cobra, it says. Thunder. On my license plates.

Sure, I say. Thunder. Great way to keep it raining. How about I name you Flood.

How about Portia, it says.

That's a girl's name, I say.

So?

You're not a girl, I say. You can't have a stick shift and be a girl.

Then why'd you get me a bra?

I remember how waiting got to be a running suicidal joke. Waiting, nine years ago, for Kirk Duncan to get my roller done and on a truck. Then, once I had it going, waiting four months for the Lodi Welding Museum to do suspension work and roll bars. Waiting six months for the Museum of Classic Auto Upholstery to give it an interior. Riding out a spring and summer waiting for a quack self-described Porsche mechanic to build a racing engine that lasted all of eighteen miles. Waiting while Wade got the specs and the parts he wanted for the replacement mill. The overnight build we did, with Dave Betts and Rocky Cimbrec, at Wade's shop in Dingman's Ferry. The name we gave it that night and the paper vanity plate that Rocky improvised. Wait. Like grade school kids, sticking a Kick Me sign on some kid we hated, we stuck it on its rear where it wouldn't know we'd done it. Now, in the garage, still waiting like it has all spring and summer for the rain to stop, it shames me to remember what we did that night, the way we laughed behind its back.

We'll name you, I say. We'll burn your bra. Get your odometer going. Play that Santana song you like. Like the old days. I promise.

The door from the house opens before it can answer me. Toni comes out. As always, it ends the conversation, because the Speedster never talks when she's around.

"Who are you talking to?" she says.

"Danny," I tell her.

"Where is he?"

"In my head."

She takes a look inside my ear. "Hi, Danny," she says.

The Volvo Guy

Sometimes I use this column to needle my buddy Paul. You may recall the guy I ran across in Carlisle, the Volvo guy, the year they hoisted and torched that sacrificial red Fiero in an automotive manifestation of Burning Man. Paul was the guy who'd maxed out his Volvo for all the safety he could dyno out of it. Everything was air bagged, from its gearshift to its radio knobs, door handles, cup holders, and vanity mirrors. This year, when Hoss Hallstrand's magic Stetson took us on an escalator ride down to the netherworld of a retro California beach, there Paul was again, the Volvo guy with the white nose, dodging the coconuts Harold Pace kept chucking down at him. I can't help myself. When you need to reach for a cheap laugh, Volvo guys are almost as easy as Citroen guys, who are as easy as picking Budweisers out of a NASCAR cooler. Two brand new Gothenburg rides occupy Paul's driveway. His is a new S80. His wife Gloria's is a new C70 droptop. In fact, Volvos litter the road of his automotive life back to his adolescence, where a 1966 Volvo 122 station wagon served as the sacrificial platform for his learning how to drive. It also acquainted him with Volvo's original safety feature, the no-race feature that gives you an ugly bang out back, and then stalls, when you try to rev the engine and drop the clutch.

But there's more to Paul than safety. For one, he's a guitarist, playing since the fourth grade, not some three-chord wonder, but a guy who knows all the tough underlying stuff about structure, harmonic and tonal theory, and the difference between dorian and mixolydian. He's the smokin' lead guitarist of this informal jazz and blues and gospel group whose members include, among others, bassist Bill Crowe and trombonist Wycliffe Gordon, professionals whose recording and performance credentials are peppered with Stan Getz, Marian McPartland, Wynton Marsalis, the Lincoln Center, Carnegie Hall. Paul owns and plays six guitars, electric and acoustic, six and twelve string, from an Epiphone personally autographed by Les Paul to a Gibson Les Paul Custom, a couple of high-end Yamahas, and two Surf City axes. As a soloist he does everything from the Beatles to the Boss. And talk about a roadie. This guy hits concerts the way I do my liquor store. BB King, the Allman Brothers, U2, Paul McCartney, Les Paul, Eric Clapton, the Cream reunion, the Police, Jethro Tull. Springsteen at least a dozen times. In summers he heads for Tennessee with a group from his church to teach, feed, and work with impoverished rural kids and improve living conditions for the hill folk. This summer they built a porch and a handicap ramp on a single-wide for a woman named Grace Bible. Finally, there's more to his automotive stable than Volvos. There's a 1965 Satellite convertible he annually runs out to the Chryslers at Carlisle weekend. He bought it because his grandfather's last car was a Satellite. Everything this guy pursues, it seems, has deep roots in his youth.

So what's he doing here, in *KCB*, instead of *Volvo Driver*, or *Guitar World*, or *Appalachia Magazine*, or *Mopar Muscle*? Well, that's because he also has deep roots in this lunatic hobby we share. Way back in the frontier days of 1982, in his twenties, Paul bought a Duchess, the MGTD replica put out by Classic Roadsters Limited, and built it in nine months. December of this year will mark 27 years since he first backed it out of his garage into a snowstorm. In 1989, the day after Thanksgiving, six inches of snow on the ground, he and Gloria made it their wedding coach. From Jersey, he's had the Duchess west as far as Cincinnati for the first ever SCVA national show, to Indiana to run laps around the Indianapolis Motor Speedway, to Pocono Raceway, and all over New England. On Connecticut's roads, with Gloria navigating, Paul drove the Duchess to a rookie first place finish in the One Lap for Kids rally. Danger has bonded them. Coming home from Indianapolis the Duchess carried him through the worst rain he's ever driven. And it's never left him stranded. Don't ask him if it's real. He'll just laugh.

Paul was there too, back in 1991, when Tim Lewis arranged a get-together one stormy day in a north Jersey park to charter the New Jersey Replicar Club. He's been Treasurer and President. I met him ten years later. This tall trim-looking dude with an almost shaved head and this take-no-prisoners exuberance for anything that came his way. Through the nineties he and the Duchess were regulars at the Carlisle Nationals. For a while there he also drove a Jovi Mercedes SL 600 rebody of a Chrysler LeBaron. For years he made all the hotel and restaurant arrangements for the club. In that famous scene in the banquet room of the old Carlisle Best Western, the club dinner where the regular kitchen crew had all walked out and the manager had rallied a bunch of off-shift pump jockeys, hairdressers, chimney sweeps, and mini-mart cashiers to cook for us, Paul was the guy who finally hollered "Enough" at his lipstick-smeared glass, and kicked down the door on his way to strangle a refund out of the manager. Always good-natured, with this boundless appetite for a good time, it's the one time I've seen him mad. Jekyll and Hyde mad.

I recently learned what his day gig is. Years ago he and Gloria went to work for a small company that did statistical and actuarial research for insurance companies. They're both executive officers now. And the company has evolved well beyond its original business. They manage secure databases for the FBI, the Department of Homeland Security, and other national law enforcement agencies. They do predictive modeling for hurricane and earthquake exposure. They can tell you the odds that your office building in Des Moines will be the target of a terrorist attack and, if it is, how much you stand to lose. They can tell you to the two-by-four what it would take to rebuild your house, to the dollar what it would cost to replace the contents, to the exact model of your bedroom TV. I ask him if he can tell what's in my closet. You know the closet. The one we all keep padlocked. He doesn't answer. That's where I get it. Paul can hurt me. Not that he would. But he can train the actuarial crosshairs, the predictive gunsights, the data-gnawing Rottweilers of his company on me, on my dark closet, on the bodies I hide in there. It should be enough to keep me from calling him the Volvo guy. I don't know if it will be. But I want to clear the record now. His vanity mirrors aren't air bagged. He's never had his Volvo on a safety dyno. He's never painted his nose white. In fact, if I could revisit that retro afternoon on the beach, I'd wipe off his nose, hand him his Gibson, stand him in with the Beach Boys, put a Hendrix Flair Hair Visor on his head, and have him play these riffs between verses of Surfin' USA that would drop your jaw around your ankles.

2010

Veterans Day

This year marks twenty years since Rocky built his CMC Speedster and started driving it. Over time, the red gelcoat has faded to hazed pink, rust has started lining the wheels, and constant patches to the wiring have left the harness looking like multi-colored dreadlocks beaded with a thousand splices. Rocky's been talking paint for years. And new wheels. And redoing the interior. And for years he's been collecting parts like acorns for the long winter of the big restoration. What scared him into finally kicking it off was finding a serious crack in the framehead. Last winter he got started. Gutted the body and pulled it off the tired pan. Picked up a reconditioned pan. In March, when he needed help fitting the old shell to the new pan, he recruited Alan and me. I asked my fifteen-year-old nephew if he wanted to come along. Hang out with some car guys. Like me, his name is Max, because both of us were named after my dad. When he was younger, around ten, he talked about being a hippie and hiding fried chicken in his hair. He doesn't like to be reminded.

Unlike Rocky, who did a tour as a helicopter mechanic, I never did Vietnam. Me and some buddies signed up for the Army Reserve our senior year in high school. We wanted to be tankers. After basic at Ord, and armor school at Knox, we came home to do our weekend warrior thing and spend two weeks each June in the Mojave, racing tanks across the lake beds, shooting up the mountains. All we knew about Vietnam was that Kennedy had stationed some "advisors" there and that monks would douse themselves with gas and sit there blazing on a city street. Within three years, of course, Vietnam was everywhere.

When we got to Rocky's, the shell of his Speedster was sitting on jackstands out on his gravel driveway. Behind it, on twenty-year-old tires, stood the old chassis, rusted from endless rainstorms and eighteen Jersey winters in the snow. The new pan was waiting in the garage. What we were there to do looked simple. Take the front beam, steering box, and tranny off the old pan, bolt them on the new one, drop the body over everything. Well, in car guy talk, the word "simple" is the funniest one-word joke there ever was. Hard scabs of old sealant were left in the nooks and crannies inside the body. Rocky handed Max a scraper. This kid, a lanky five foot nine, took a drop light, folded himself up in the footwell like a paper clip, and got to work, while three old guys stood there watching, trying not to remember the last time they were that limber. Two yokes on the new pan had to be strengthened before we could mount the beam. Alan went after them. The nose cone on the tranny was wrong for the new pan. Rocky took a two-hour run to a place that had the right one. I repacked the old IRS hubs and found that the rubber boots were shot.

They never called our unit up for Vietnam. I never knew why. It was crazy. We were trained. We were combat ready. They were using tanks in Vietnam. Instead, kids my age and two or three years younger were getting drafted, putting their cars on blocks, quitting their jobs, casing their guitars, hoping their girlfriends would stay put, saying goodbye to a frame of reference they didn't know they wouldn't be returning to. Under the long cloud of that war, while kids I knew angled for deferments, sweated through lotteries, joined two-year lines for National Guard openings, while other kids I knew were coming home in boxes, crippled, disfigured in other ways, I got married, went to engineering classes, rebuilt and raced an old Speedster, graduated, kept doing the weekend warrior thing. One guy I'd worked with on a mobile home assembly line came home when a bouncing Betty took his groin out. He took what they called his "compensation" pay and paid cash for a brand new Super Bee. A drummer buddy came home and could never keep time again. Me? I beat Vietnam. Not on purpose. Not knowing why. But I did.

So I thought. Two of the thousands of guys who fought that war were named Phillip and Jim. Phillip was from Queens. He was Toni's first husband. He came home with his face and head riddled with shrapnel. They had a daughter and a son, Desiree and Damon, but within a few years he was gone. By the time I met Toni, without any kids of my own, hers were in their teens, and I had to come up to speed on fatherhood fast. Jim was from Indiana. He did three Navy tours in Vietnam, running patrol boats up and down the rivers, jumping in to swim around and draw fire out of the jungles. He and my sister were married in the late eighties. They had a daughter, and later on a son, and then Jim got cancer, a rare and unbeatable form that his doctors wrote up to Agent Orange exposure, and a year and a half later he was gone too. Max was two and his sister Sophie five. I was their new main man.

At Rocky's we broke for lunch. Max got asked to pass around some of that fried chicken he was hiding in his hair. We ended up with sandwiches. And got back to work. Max scraped some sealant away from the bottom corner of the doorframe and twenty years of dirt and gravel started sifting out. Out came the air gun and shop vac. We got the front beam on but Alan had to resection part of the framehead to level it. We got the tranny in but couldn't get the shift rod right. Max kept getting the tight and twisted jobs. Over the course of the afternoon I sensed the change in him. He wasn't there with his uncle. He was there on his own. Because we needed him. He stopped waiting to be told what to do next. He caught the rhythm of the teamwork. He started to anticipate where he was needed and jump in on his own.

How do you thank two guys — two veterans who lost their lives to a war you never fought — for giving you a family? For the human wealth of their four great kids? I don't know. You keep butting up against the truth that they deserve to be here. That the place you hold is theirs. And then all you can do is hope that you do right by them. We finally picked the body up, one car guy at each wheelwell, stumbled it inside, hoisted it up and over the chassis. There were still a million "simple" things to do before Rocky could seat it. But we'd done what we'd come for. We left toward dusk. In the passenger seat, asleep in the light of the dash, Max took home a set of grit black fingernails and a headful of car guy stories his buddies couldn't start to hold a candle to.

For Real

"Where'd they go?"

Warm and cloudless Saturday afternoon. A no-brainer. "They're at the Station House, out on the deck, suckin' down Yuenglings in the sun."

I'm in the garage with Danny Piperato's 550 Spyder. Danny drove it down from New York to help the guy who owns me fix a miss in my engine. He made room in the garage to have Danny park the Spyder next to me. Then, while Danny's Spyder watched, they opened my engine lid, jacked my rear end in the air, and got to work back there. I don't know what they did. But it was embarrassing, all jacked up, everything hanging out, in front of this famous car I'd heard about but never met before. They worked away for a while, then took me out on a test run where the miss popped up again, and then they got to where they needed gaskets or toothpaste or mayonnaise or something and all the parts shops were locked for the weekend. So they closed me up and let me down. And then they took off. And a couple minutes later Danny's Spyder asks me where they've gone.

"Sounds about right," Danny's Spyder says. "Whaddaya say they're talkin' about all the women they ever got run over by."

"I say you just busted 'em."

"I didn't look," Danny's Spyder says, "Just so you know."

"At what?"

"At you. When they had you all jacked up and your rocker arm covers off. I don't corner that way."

"No problem," I say. "But I appreciate it."

"Nice garage. Got enough headroom for a lift."

"The guy who owns me says he'll get around to it some day."

"What's your name?" Danny's Spyder says.

"He says he'll get around to naming me too," I tell him. "What's yours?"

"Danny calls me Sleepy or Dopey. Depending on how he feels about himself. His ex called me the Last Straw. His new gal, she doesn't call me anything, but she sure likes to warm my seat up."

We both laugh at that for a minute.

"Are you real?" I ask.

"A real Spyder? You think I'd be sitting here if I was?"

"Yeah. You got me there."

"I already know you're not real."

"Lemme guess," I say. "These butt flares."

"You don't smell."

"Smell?"

"Yeah. Them old ones, man, they just smell. Like these nasty old people who wanna just be left alone and die."

"You're right, man. I was at this show once, parked there, and this real Speedster comes along and gets parked right next to me. All

I kept smelling was cabbage and ammonia."

"Yeah," says Danny's Spyder. "Probably more like that formaldehyde stuff."

"He started talking to me. Man, his breath was so sour I almost started bawling. He told me how he just wanted to go off and die but the guy who owned him wouldn't let him. He thought I was a reincarnated one. Said that's what he wanted to do. Die and come back. It was sad. I couldn't tell him you can't reincarnate a trail of rust."

"Rust, man," Danny's Spyder says. "That's nothin' but slow motion cremation."

"You couldn't get me to be a real one for a million bucks."

"Me either. All those freakin' operations. All that new metal they gotta keep puttin' in just to keep from crumblin' away."

"Yeah. And them engines that couldn't pull a Chihuahua out of a rain puddle."

"They oughta have a euthanasia law. A Dr. Kevorkian place where they could sneak off to get their lights put out."

"Yeah. But instead they keep gettin' restored, and it's all Mexican and Chinese stuff, and before long, they're about as real as we are."

"Except we're not a hundred years old. We ain't had thirty-four hundred owners and fifteen paint jobs. We ain't got french fries from 1958 down in our seat cracks."

"We ain't ready to die, either."

We sit there and consider that for a minute.

"We're not just talkin' jealous, are we?" I finally say.

We sit there and consider that possibility too.

"Hell, no," Danny's Spyder says. "Besides, I got the coolest guy who owns me in the world."

I think about the guy who owns me. He's kinda cool too. Just lets me sit around too much.

"I could use a Yuengling myself," I say.

"Maybe they'll bring us back a couple."

From there we talk about Speedsters and Spyders we've gotten to know. Then about Cobras, Divas, TDs, Allards, Lambos, other cars we hang out with. From there we get to Carlisle. I don't tell Danny's Spyder, but the last time I was there, I fell in love with this little red Mini, and she took to me too. She didn't care if I wasn't the real deal. I didn't care if she was sixty-three years older than me. She'd taken good care of herself. We had plans to see each other the next year.

Like he can read my mind almost, Danny's Spyder says, "Danny's gonna make the guy who owns you finally take you this year again."

"Not sure I still know the way."

"It'll come back."

"You ever have other cars ask you if Danny's real?"

"All the time. We'll be somewhere, they'll wait till he leaves, then they'll come up and say, is that guy real?"

"Me too," I say. "Whaddaya tell 'em?"

"Depends on who they are," says Danny's Spyder. "A Cobra, I'll say no, he's a cross between your engine builder and your left taillight. A Valkyrie, I'll say yeah, he's real, he's the King of Norway. What about you?"

"I got in a fight once when this Volvo asked me and I said yeah, he's as real as your freakin' bean sprout wiring harness. We ended up sideswipin' the crap outta each other. Shoulda seen his air bags goin' off. Like a string of firecrackers."

We keep swapping stories. Once, the door from the house opens, and there's the wife of the guy who owns me, and we shut up, and she looks around confused before she shrugs and goes back in. And then Danny and the guy who owns me are back, all loud and lit up, all cleansed and righteous like they just got baptized.

"You were right," I tell Danny's Spyder, "about all the women they got run over by."

Reconcilable Differences

A year and a half ago, my Speedster already in the long Rip Van Winkle nap from which it will finally be awakened this month, my father died. He was ninety.

He wasn't a tall man. He was stocky, muscular, built like a small bear, probably the most robust and tireless man I've ever known. He was a young father when he packed up his family and left the strictured Protestant skies of Switzerland to seek the Kingdom of God in as unlikely a place as Utah. I was four years old when we crossed the Atlantic on the Queen Elizabeth and then flew from New York to Salt Lake on an old Constellation. My grandparents had blazed the trail a year earlier. They were renting a two-story house in one of Salt Lake's original neighborhoods. For the first few months we shared its unfinished basement with three families — those of my aunts — who had also made the journey. Blankets were hung from the joists to give us privacy. From there, while my father looked for footing in a country whose language he could barely speak, we lived in apartments, duplexes, houses that today look inconceivably small, spent four years on a ranch in Southern Utah, and finally settled into one of the orchard towns in the foothills north of Salt Lake, within ten miles of the heart of the faith he had followed from Switzerland. He'd reached his destination. With three sons, and two daughters, his family was complete. It was where we would grow up. It was the one home we associate today with permanence.

He was, in many ways, a typical immigrant. The move from Switzerland unleashed boundless reserves of energy and exuberance and purpose. He embraced the country that welcomed him with incredible fervor and barefaced gratitude. He enlisted his kids in keeping the yard immaculate. He flew the Stars and Stripes. He was a great guy to have for a neighbor. He learned English on the fly, from job to job, to where his spoken and written grammar was flawless.

He embraced his faith with profound humility and consummate obedience. What his faith held out to him was the unprecedented promise of eternal togetherness for his family. He could always have us. We could always be a family. A promise that immense, of course, had to be earned. There were rules and conditions that held not only for him but for every one of us. Any of us could void that promise. Any of us could falter, break faith, and end up lost to him. And so, in the harness of that astonishing promise, he put his heart and energy into keeping the rest of us faithful, holding us together, making us the model family it would take to earn it. Doubt that he could do it only fueled his drive and vigilance. Then came the sixties. Five kids who'd worn the harness and run obediently in the traces of his faith began to discover pathways of their own. By the early seventies all five of us were gone.

He never shared my interest in cars. He hadn't grown up that way. His first car was a 52 Buick Skylark. He was in his thirties and saddled with a family when he bought it. He owned tools but could never take the time away from his job and church to learn how to use them. My first car was a used Super 90 Cabriolet. He let me drive him to work once. Later on we didn't talk about the rustbucket 55 Speedster I was salvaging. The engine I was building. The way I welded quarter inch steel up and down the rusted boxes to strengthen them, widened the wheels for fatter tires, dropped the suspension to almost zero travel, stripped out the upholstery, sandblasted the paint and putty out of the body, kept it painted with a couple of cans of red oxide primer every spring and fall. We never talked much about anything immediate. What mattered to him was winning us back. We went on to college. We launched careers. We started families. We gave him grandkids. For the next thirty to forty years, while he celebrated our secular achievements, there was always the rip tide of his restless and powerful appetite to win us back. The promise had slipped his grasp. It stood between us like a shadow, not only of our failure but of his, a constant nagging expectation that kept him from giving his blessing to the immediate reality of who we were. We could see the way it haunted him deep under the surface of his face. We could feel it in our long and often angry appetite to be acknowledged. We could sense it in the packages he mailed us after we moved away, packages of church literature and newspaper clippings promoting Salt Lake as the best place in the universe to live, packages that invoked heartbreak as much as they bred resentment.

The last ten years of his life were marked by three changes. First, after a lifetime of no manifest interest in sports, he and my mother became ardent fans of the Utah Jazz. Second, his pursuit to win us back dropped off, and a new attitude of acceptance began to define our relationship. The pursuit of that promise may simply have worn him down. Third, the once robust and tireless engine of his body started to give out. He loved to write. But he started to lose the ability to read what he was writing or what we were writing back to him. He underwent the replacement of a hip and both knees and then lived for years with a debilitating and resistant infection when one knee went bad. Toward the end, blind except for telling light from dark, his hearing started going. He spent his last few months in the hospital, and his last few days hallucinating while my kid brother held his hand.

I'd known for a long time that he and I would have to wait until he died before we could fully reconcile what stood between us. When the long shadow of our failure to meet that exacting promise was gone. When it would just be him and me. When he would know that he would always have his family. That it wasn't a promise that stood at the end of an obstacle course of rules and conditions, but as simple a human entitlement as sight and the ability to think and run and laugh. We had a lot to talk about. I had a lot to show him. I jumped right in. I showed him around the house he'd never had the opportunity to visit. I drove him around and showed him everything and every place that mattered in the area. I told him stories he'd never heard. I played Pat Metheny for him. I took him along on errands. It took two solid weeks to acquaint him with my life and talk through everything. Sometimes it got heated. He understood this. I still talk to him each day. I know he's there because this sense of peace I've lately had is new and has his name all over it.

I'm sure he's already been out in the garage to take a gander at the Speedster for himself. But I'm saving showing him the car I built until I've knocked the dust off, until it's up and running, until I can show him everything, until I can take him for a run through the hills and farmlands of the part of Jersey they call God's country.

Cry if I Want to

This is a true story. Lately, there's been a man who follows me everywhere I go, points me out to people, and tells them it's my birthday. I never see him. I don't know what he looks like. I couldn't recognize him in a lineup of saltwater fish. I just know he's there, because I've had strangers come up to me and say "Happy Birthday," and when I've asked them how they knew, they've said, "That guy back there told me." Then, when we've turned around to look, they've said, "That's funny. He was right there." At other times, I'll hear people behind me break out in song, and sure enough, there in the blank toward the end, they'll holler out my name. So he knows who I am, this man, and he always knows where I'm going. Heading across a parking lot toward Staples, KFC, Sears. Stopping for gas to have my man from Pakistan behind the counter hand me a new Bic lighter and say, "For your birthday, my friend." At cruise nights I'll have a guy with a slammed 49 Merc or 427 Cobra hand me the keys and tell me it's mine for the weekend. Sometimes I'll just have a woman give me this little smile. For a minute there I think wow. I've still got it. But no. The smile's for an old guy on his birthday. Sometimes, out with Toni at a restaurant, seventeen waitresses will suddenly swarm around us, plant a slice of carrot cake in front of me, and start singing their nubile hearts out. They always know my name too.

"This is getting creepy," Toni has started saying.

"Tell me," I always say, because I don't know what else to say.

"You think it's Gus?" she says, using our son's chance nickname for a previous girl in my life. "You said she was big on birthdays."

"Nah," I say. "People always say they heard it from a guy."

"Maybe she hired him."

Neighbors, people around town, clients, even folks I used to drink with twenty years ago send me cards at the strangest times. Flowers and balloons show up at random. Crazy Steve, my buddy across the street, calls me every week or two and says, "Hey, man, happy birthday. I thought you just had one." "Yeah," I say, because I don't know what else to say. "I just keep being reborn." My neighbor Ruth thinks I'm 900 years old. My nephew calls me Uncle Methuselah. At least, except for the eight hundred lighters my man from Pakistan has given me, I don't get presents. That would be another story. One I'd be writing from jail.

I've disguised myself. Painted my windows black on the inside. Held a yard sale to prove I own nothing of value. Changed my brand of cereal. Dug a tunnel to the back yard next door. Even left the country. But distance doesn't faze this guy. He travels light. Last winter, in a Mexican restaurant somewhere in the Dominican Republic, it happened again. I'm having dinner with the Tropical Ten when suddenly a cupcake festooned with blazing sparklers is planted right in front of me, and just as suddenly four waiters, seven waitresses, and the kitchen staff are gathered round, belting out Happy Birthday while my eyebrows catch fire and QueenBee has to throw her mojito in my face to put them out. My real birthday is five months off. But I go along. These are friends. You don't diminish the experience by telling them your birthday happens every day. You don't ruin it by telling them it's a mistake and then passing your driver's license around to prove it. You go along. You act surprised and overwhelmed.

Then comes Carlisle. Toni and I don't get there till late Friday afternoon. We planned on arriving earlier but stopped at a Burger King just past Allentown for lunch and got ambushed by another birthday party. When we finally got to the hotel, still wearing our paper crowns, the parking lot was a lively reunion of Speedster folks and their Speedsters. I feared the worst. But they were just happy to see us. There wasn't a whiff of anything remotely related to a birthday.

Things were quiet that night. On Saturday, at the show field, things were quiet too. I didn't trust it. Would a Marilyn Monroe look-alike jump out of Hoss Hallstrand's ten-gallon hat and sing Happy Birthday Mr. President? Would the Volvo Guy give me a bouquet of air bags painted up and filled with helium? Would Bob Hess the Rust Doctor have my secret high school love waiting for me in the back seat of a time-traveling Shoebox Ford? Would Carey Hines give me an all-expenses-paid day at the Indiana Disneyland of the Special Edition factory? None of that happened. There was the sacrificial Fiero, out in an empty field, waiting to be hoisted and torched later that night on the pyre of a mile-high hydraulic lift. The usual people were coming out of Building X, sunburned from an afternoon on Bruce Meyers' netherworld beach, still humming Kingston Trio tunes. Nothing. Just a usual Saturday in which I was happy to pass for an invisible guy whose birthday was nobody's business.

If it ended there, of course, this wouldn't be a story. That night we join a hundred Speedster folks and guests for a traditional dinner in a private room at Sunnyside Restaurant. I figure I'm safe. The day is over. I'm among friends. I carelessly start knocking back drinks. Wolf down a salmon and crabmeat special. Look forward to Cory Drake's photo presentation. The waitress clears away my plate. The tablecloth stays vacant. I figure I'm good. But not for long. It's not much as cakes go. I've seen bigger hubcaps on a Pinto, and there's only one candle where, at last count, there should be over a thousand. But it's a cake. No avoiding that. Across the table, my pals Kim and Norma kick off the song I can hear in my fingernails now, and by the time they're two bars in, the whole place is singing, stomping their feet, clapping. I've never heard that many people sing the same song at the same time since the last time I went to church about 640 years ago. What do you do? Tell a hundred well-meaning friends and acquaintances who've just sung their lungs inside out and pounded their hands raw that it's really not your birthday? That they've just been hoodwinked? That somewhere there's a sick man laughing? No. You hang your head. You act humbled as the false object of all the real but misplaced affection.

Who are you? Do you even know my real birthday? Are you being paid for this? Do you have a life? Are you going for some Guinness or Ripley's thing? Why me? Do you want my Speedster? Will you take my wife instead? What did I do to you? If you're the son I never knew I had, hey, just take me on the Maury Show, and we'll settle it there. If you're a student I flunked 20 years ago for never showing up in class, hey, let me know, and I'll leave you an A in my will. I don't care. Show yourself. Talk to me. We'll work it out. I'm getting way too old for this.

Getting Ants Drunk

They drop out of the tree overhead, land on the glass top of the table, start scurrying around. It's after work, and Toni and I are sitting out on the deck, relaxing with a couple of Malibu Rums while we watch them. On the circular flat earth of the tabletop, they look like they're hunting for food, so I dip my finger and flick a drop of rum on the table. In a few seconds one of them darts into it by accident. Whoa. What's this. Watching it, I ponder the surface tension of a drop of Malibu Rum, and wonder how much strength it takes an ant to pierce it. Half a minute later, it backs away, turns a couple of circles, looks around, stops and rubs its face, and then finds its way back.

Except for being terrified as a kid by the giant ones that came shrieking out of the desert heat in the old movie *Them*, and for exterminating them for not paying rent, I've never much related to ants. So what happens next is astonishing. My vision zeroes in and sharpens. For the first time, watching it suck down the same thing I'm drinking, I'm seeing the intricate articulation of an ant's body —

its stomach, its rear end, the tiny anvil of its head — in a way I never have. When it moves back a second time, and rears up a little stunned, I'm seeing the finely jointed filaments of its legs, and when it rubs its face again, I'm imagining hands, too small for the naked eye to see. It reacts to rum just like I do. In the haze of the late afternoon, under mixed clouds, I realize what I'm doing. I'm empathizing with a tree ant. I'm turning it into a tiny man. Watching it get itself drunk, I'm seeing my own behavior, knowing exactly what it's going through. Then, just the way I would, and at the same exact time, it goes back for a third hit. When it finally pulls its face out of the drop again, it meanders an inch or two off, then drops in its tracks and stays there. To my left, Toni is watching too, and she's worried it may be dead. Not so. She taps a fingernail on the glass an inch or two away. It jumps to its feet, looks wildly around, then lies down and goes quiet again.

"He's passed out," says Toni.

When she calls it a "he," I know she's had the same transcendent experience I've just had.

"He's sleeping it off," I say.

In the meantime, another ant has bellied up to the same drop. I'm suddenly a bartender. I flick him a drop of his own. Some guys golf. I could spend my retirement doing this.

Sitting here, getting two ants drunk, I'm imagining what it would take for an ant to build a Cobra. Hey. They're industrious and smart. They're into teamwork. I don't doubt for a minute that they could. It's mostly a question of scale and material. Can fiberglass be made that small and retain its properties? Can the molecular structure of metal hold up when it's drawn into a brake line as fine as a human hair? How about rubber? Could bias ply work for a tire so tiny you'd need a microscope to read that it's made by Goodyear? Is a 427 Sideoiler the size of a fishing sinker possible? What would you use instead of horsepower? Can gasoline be atomized in a Weber no bigger than a pinhead? Gauges? Valves? If you apply nanotechnology to our hobby, is its future a Cobra an ant could build and drive to a car show?

"Honey?"

"Yeah. I'm back."

"Do you think we could get arrested for this? By the SPCA?"

"Maybe we shoulda checked IDs."

That's the kind of afternoon it is, hot, humid, the trees exhausted, the lines of hills and ridges off the deck out in front of us dissolving into haze, nothing holding much reality. I figure it's a good time to set the record straight on some things I've left unanswered on this page. In a recent column about my father I mentioned that his first car was a 1952 Buick Skylark. My friend Sandy Fox, who spent his career in the automotive industry, wrote to let me know that Buick didn't make a Skylark then. Most likely it was a Special. I've ridiculed my buddy Paul as the Volvo Guy when he's never owned a Volvo in his life. Other people I've used in this column simply don't exist. Rocky, Danny, and Alan the Car Whisperer are figments of my imagination, cobbled-together portraits of friends I wish I had, their women no more than computer-matured holograms of Playmates I remember. This afternoon, even Toni seems unreal, and the Speedster in my garage is just a rusted-out vintage Lancia I'm storing for my plumber. Sitting here, I don't know anyone named Hoss, or Lane, or Gordon, or Cory, or Pineapplehead Jim or Rocket Scientist Kelly any more than the ant still napping on my table, or the second one taking a breather now, or the three new ants I've just served. But then it doesn't matter, because on an afternoon like this, when I open it and look for what I could swear I wrote, even this magazine evaporates and leaves me looking at my hands.

"Your little bar is getting busy," Toni says.

I'm remembering the way *Them* ended. The giant ants invaded the sewers of Los Angeles where they were cornered and torched with flamethrowers.

"Yeah," I say. "Why don't you cover for me for a while."

"Sure."

"I'll take another drink too," I say. "While you're at it."

Their barstools are tiny. Most of them, like me, choose to stand. They don't talk to each other much, which surprises me, because they're car ants, and their Bugattis, Cobras, GT40s, Speedsters, Lambos, Hi-Boys, Spyders, Divas, MGs, shoebox Fords, and rock climbers are inches away in the parking lot. We should be talking up a storm. Out in the lot, a couple of ants are bent over fenders like they're looking under each other's hoods, but when I focus in, they're just chucking their Malibu cookies into somebody else's engine bay. Been there.

"Be careful," I say. "They gotta drive home."

"You need to get out of the heat," says Toni. "It's closing time anyway."

Sometimes, aside from the woman named Norma I met in a Baltimore airport hotel where we were waiting out a blizzard, the only thing real is this: the stuff that isn't. Toni's using her napkin to wipe the bar clean. The ants that aren't passed out are confused, then alarmed, and then they're just unhappy. In the path of her napkin they try to suck down what's left. They rear up, shake their tiny fists, and I can feel the flex of their knuckles in my own hands, because my drink's gone too, and I'm being chased away while the sun's still up along with the rest of them, left standing in the parking lot with the key to my Speedster in my hand, blinking and bewildered like I've just walked out of a matinee of *Them* into the blazing paint and catalyzed exhaust of rush hour traffic.

A Guy on the Sidewalk

For much of the eighties I lived in Manhattan. I'd been in the East a couple of years, had always contemplated heading back to Utah, but figured I'd always regret it if I went home without giving the city a shot. I was also in love with an East Coast girl. So I sold my 65 Pontiac Catalina and tools to a high school kid and my Mustang II to a nurse for the cash to rent a small studio apartment on East 30th Street. Luckily the room had a ceiling high enough to build a second floor. I mounted it seven feet high on four-by-four posts, joisted and planked and painted it, built a shelf off the back for a fan, and threw a mattress, some books, two lamps, and a clock radio up there. A folding stepladder got us up and down. And then we were New Yorkers. Our place was four blocks down and two across from the Empire State Building, two blocks north of Little India and a fast food joint called "Curry in a Hurry," a couple of long blocks from the East River. A few stops down on the Lexington IRT and we were in the Village. A couple of uptown stops put us in Central Park. A walk across town and we were at the Javits Center, home of the

New York Auto Show, where I saw my first replica Speedster, a black CMC California.

An auto show on an island where most everyone was a pedestrian always struck me as an oxymoron. It would have been one thing if it consisted of the newest crop of garbage trucks and yellow Caprices — the donor car of choice at the time for New York cabs — and the Tauruses the rental car industry went for. But no. It was a full-blown show, complete with Diablos, dizzying concept cars, everything. The only vehicles that made sense, given the city's streets, were the armored-looking off-road trucks. Other than that, it was like staging a yacht show in the Sahara, or putting a Kansas pig farm in downtown Tel Aviv. What made the least sense, of course, was that black CMC, and the salesman who kept trying to sell me one, even after I told him I'd sold all my tools and lived in a studio apartment the size of a master bedroom in a mobile home.

Winter was coming on when we moved there. I remember sitting in a window table of a place down on Eighth Avenue called the White Horse. Snow was floating down and catching soft white fire in the streetlights and headlights. I worried reflexively about getting us home. Nobody else much seemed to care. And then it hit me. I was a pedestrian. For the first time in years there wasn't a car key on my key ring. No snow tires. No swerving ride. No blood alcohol level to care about. We could walk, jump a subway, or just step outside, pull a cab off Eighth Avenue, tell the guy where we lived. I wrote our address down in case I got to where I couldn't remember it. And then I had another drink.

At first it was the novel experience I expected. We found a neighborhood bar up the street and started using it as our living room along with regulars we started seeing as our family. Mets and

Yankees games. Jazz in the Village. Simon and Garfunkel, the Lennon vigil, Shakespeare in Central Park. Broadway. I saw Cats ten times just to see if the nine lives thing was true. Prince and Tina Turner at the Garden. Ashford and Simpson, Luther Van Dross, Jimmy Buffet at Radio City. Like me, most everyone was from somewhere else, so I fit right in. But the saying "faster than a New York minute" is true. Time flies in that town. What started as a whim — trying out the Apple before heading back West — turned into a Groundhog Day of repeating seasons. Before long I'd accrued five years that felt like one. I was hanging out with guys in their thirties who'd never had a driver's license, something that made no sense, like never getting whiskers or having your voice change. My own license might as well have been a Social Security card for all the use it got. I was walking or being hauled wherever I went. Getting out of town meant running the gauntlet of Grand Central, Penn Station, or Port Authority with a million other pedestrians. The city itself was changing. Trump ruled. "Needle" buildings were going up on vacant lots the size of sandboxes. Yuppie investment bankers were forcing artists and writers and musicians and actors out of town across the rivers to Jersey and the outer boroughs. The Village clubs that offered jazz were disappearing. Power broads — suited-up chicks with fresh MBAs and briefcases — were tailgating me down the sidewalks on the hard crack of their angry heels. The city was losing its soul. It felt less like America than an Alcatraz for the rich. Looking west, I'd watch the sun go down through a canyon of buildings, wishing I could follow it.

I finally bought a car as a way to get out of town without a train ticket and a thousand strangers along for the ride. Before long, to break the drowning grip of the city, I was taking midnight rides.

Down the FDR, across the Brooklyn Bridge, out the Belt Parkway, over the Verrazano, across Staten Island, the Bayonne Bridge into Jersey, up the Turnpike, back into town through the Holland Tunnel. The loop took under an hour, the windows down, the Manhattan skyline off to my right the entire ride, a brief reprieve from a place where the thesis "Why I live here" was resulting in shorter and shorter essays. I wanted to live where I could walk out my door and see my car parked in a driveway. I wanted to sleep where I couldn't reach up and touch the ceiling. I wanted tools. I wanted that CMC. I wanted snow I had to be careful about. A blood alcohol level I had to watch. When the real estate boom finally took down our neighborhood bar, my last reason to stick around was gone.

Years ago, heading west on 80, there was a billboard just as you crossed the Delaware River into Pennsylvania that read "Welcome to America." I didn't agree. Northwest Jersey qualified too. But it had been seven years. And what they say about riding a bike didn't hold true for driving. Winding roads intimidated me. I slowed down for curves a quarter mile early and then crawled around them like black ice was possible in July. The feel for driving had to be earned again. Once it was back I took it the other way. I was the Amish kid in a Lancaster bar, fresh off the compound for the first time, unleashed, reckless, ignorant of the social mores everyone else knew enough to get along on. I welcomed curves with suicidal relish. I clipped a Passport to my visor and drove like a red-eyed banshee. I threw vein-popping tantrums in the driver's seat. I left tooth marks in the steering wheel. Everything on the road had to be chased down and passed. There were some real Jesus-take-the-wheel episodes before I learned how to fit in and go easy. I own tools again. And while it isn't a CMC, or black, I've got a replica Speedster. But the scars of pedestrianism remain. I continue to be averse to walking or being driven anywhere unless it's by Danny in his Spyder. And when I drive into Manhattan, knowing that well before dark I'll be back in America, I look for that guy on the sidewalk and wonder. Seven years. How it happened.

2011

Running the Pumpkin

His name is Kelly and he's a bona fide rocket scientist. Some time ago, looking to tile his bathroom, faced with some complicated cuts, he calls a rental place and asks if they have a tile saw. They do. When he gets there the counter guy takes him in back. One would have been easy. But they've got three of them, lined up, ranging in size and, figures Kelly, application. Standing there like Goldilocks he starts rattling off the parameters of his job to the counter guy. Tile size, thickness, density, shear strength, bevel cuts, miter joints, worksite temperature and humidity, his expertise at tiling. Obviously the counter guy's never rented one himself. He stands there, shrugging off Kelly's questions, as paralyzed as Kelly by the possibilities. Well, he finally says, it ain't rocket science. I know it's not, Kelly tells him gently, because if it was, I'd have it figured out by now. Don't tell me, the counter guy says, and hangs his head.

Kelly's telling me this story on a warm October morning in Pennsylvania on the deck of the Kim and Alan Merklin home in Chambersburg. Nothing beats seeing a convoy of Speedsters still raw with road wind come cruising down the street of an unassuming neighborhood whose only wish is to be left alone. A while ago, Kelly's was one of them, Babs in the passenger seat, pulling up on the Merklin grass. Two MGTDs and some other Speedsters have also joined the party. Down below us, Wild Bill, Calamity Joan, Ed, Karen, Norma, Bruce, Wolfgang, Barry, Toni, Dale, Linda, Rocky, Lewis, Cory, Alan, Kim, and Justin and his dad are milling around, checking out each other's latest innovations, swapping road stories. I'm wondering if shoe clubs do this. Cory's checkered flag doo-rag makes him easy to spot. The Hoopty, his silver and orange clamshell Speedster, stands out like a pit bull at poodle school.

We're here for the third annual Pumpkin Run, courtesy of Kim and the Car Whisperer, so named because it's that time of year and the Pennsylvania farmland is peppered with them, orange gourds marking autocross courses only a gopher could follow. Kim and Alan have passed out bagels, fruit, coffee. Alan and his neighbor Doug have put together an 80-mile route that will take in some historic Pennsylvania towns, lots of rolling country, a museum of Amish cookware, a mountaintop, and a joint called Dilly's. We're ready to roll.

Alan leads the way in Kim's Miata with Rocky riding shotgun. Kim and Linda, their dispensable wives when it's boy time, are safely out of reach of being remembered, caged in Kim's Accord, the next-to-last car in the convoy. Behind them, in a cherry red Corvette, Doug and Shirley are doing sweep duty to keep the herd together. We're toward the rear too, in Toni's S2000, Toni driving.

Lined up ahead of us are the real cars. Seven Speedsters and two TDs. The round rear end of Cory's Hoopty is just in front of us. I was wrong earlier. What beats watching a convoy of Speedsters crack the morning quiet of a neighborhood is being on the move with them, watching them roll along the easy undulations of the low hills, stretch out on the snaking curves, high on the unburned carburetor gas in their exhaust, the eager collective orchestra of their engines playing on the wind. The sky is cloudless, the weather in the seventies, the leaves just starting to turn.

Parts of Pennsylvania can take my breath the way they evoke Europe. Back when I was twenty, I drove the same kinds of roads in Austria, in a borrowed Beetle and a missionary suit, dreaming of coming back one day and doing them in a Porsche with someone more amorously promising than a farm kid from Idaho in the passenger seat. Today's that kind of day. Today, if I squint just enough to blur out the occasional Blazer or Ford F-10 coming the other way, the English writing on the signs, and the Miata out in front, I'm back there, living that getaway European dream, touring with European friends who share it. Apple Valley becomes a little southern border town named Villach. Ellenville becomes Knittelfeld. Green Castle becomes Eisenerz. In the fields the pumpkins speak a lazy German dialect. Norma is Heidi, Alan is Franz, Kim is Steffi, Big Dale is Leopold, Kelly is Einstein, Justin is Karl, his dad Heinz. Wolfgang stays Wolfgang. But Cory's checkered doo-rag and rawboned Speedster make him a ringer for Manfred von Richthofen. Trolling through a town that on any other day would be Mercersburg, but for today is Klagenfurt, church bells are clamoring for us, and an Austrian cop with the heart of a car guy steps out and holds traffic back so that Alan and Rocky can't ditch the rest of us.

We leave the valleys for the mountains. We stop at the Birthplace of James Buchanan, a dirt turnaround in the woods, the cabin where he came into the world howling to be elected moved to a location more accessible to midwives. From there, we're chasing up mountain switchbacks, then doing a low-dust mosey up a dirt road to the summit, a craggy overlook with a fifty-mile view spread out around us. A group of young hikers are sunning their nether parts on the rocks and feeding each other raisins and pistachios. It's still Austria, so everyone's cool, but the snapping red eye of Rocky's cell phone makes them put their clothes on. Hawks and turkey vultures float on the air below us. I ask Doug what we're looking at. He spools off mountains and valleys with historic names like Shenandoah. Soon we're moseying back to asphalt, then screaming off the mountain, a kamikaze squadron diving for the valley floor. Back in Chambersburg, we hijack the deck of the joint called Dilly's for food, drink, and a surprise party for my 748th birthday. Toni buys the table a round of Jose Cuervo shots. I tell Baron von Richthofen I want a doo-rag for my birthday. Never ceasing to amaze me, Cory gets up, takes his off, hands it to me. I try it on and hand it back. No, he says. It's yours. Back on it goes.

We say goodbye to folks like Ed and Karen who need to get home before their cars — you guessed it — start turning back to pumpkins. The rest of us head for the Merklin place, where a strawberry pie with a candle, another round of shots, and yet another chorus of my signature song are waiting to turn me another year older. Outside, off the deck, oil spots from the morning gathering mark the grass. Wild Bill steps out. Lookin' good for 749 there, he says, and asks me how I do it. I've just done Austria. I'm wearing Cory's gift of his checkered doo-rag. I'm way past caring. Well, I tell him, it ain't rocket science, or Kelly would have it figured out by now.

Jimmy

He was this rambling ragtag happy-go-lucky street guy who was always around the neighborhood of 30th Street. He wore busted-out workboots, no laces, and he walked with this huge goofy swinging stride that made me think of Johnny Appleseed. And he moved. Full of purpose, like he had somewhere to go, he'd weave through people with the easy grace of a sailplane, his big tan canvas overcoat riding the wind he left behind him. His hair was this standout mop of dusty electrocuted-looking dreadlocks. He was the happiest guy I knew. In a city where you didn't openly grin, he was always grinning, this big meaty grin that animated his entire face, and his laugh was always there, ready to go, an engine quietly but eagerly idling back behind his grin. Just call me Jimmy, he said, when I asked. He never asked back. One day, light rain falling, I ran into him on 31st. He was using a small bright yellow umbrella with a couple of busted spokes and a chrome stub of a handle to keep his dreads dry. In the weird light underneath it, the ledges of his brown skin took on highlights of iridescent green, and I realized that he'd started to call me Ricky.

He was from Virginia. I figured a small town because that was the feel he gave a neighborhood that didn't have much feel — like a block or two away, in any direction, there could be an orchard, a field, a shady place to drop a fishing line. Our conversations were brief, on the surface, so I never knew much else. How he made his way to New York. Where he lived. If or where he worked. I never saw him panhandle. I knew he didn't deal. I could tell he had a place to shave. But he wore that overcoat year round — even in the thick heat of July — and I figured it was because he didn't have a place secure enough to hang it. From there it was easy to figure that everything he owned was in its pockets. But I never knew how tough his life might be. It never showed. It never marked him. Nothing cut the spirit of his grin when he saw you coming half a block away, or stalled that ready laugh, or slowed that Johnny Appleseed stride, not even the unforgiving January winds that howled down the long canyons of the Avenues. It was a rare day when I didn't run into him or hear him holler from across the street. I told him once if he ever needed help to ask me. He looked surprised and then curious. I never brought it up again.

I only saw him twice without his hallmark grin. The first was the day Tom Carvel died. He took it hard. The second was a Monday three years into our street-bound friendship. It was hot. One of those days when the year stagnates in the backwash of August. He couldn't look at me. I'd never seen him evasive. I asked what was up. He asked shyly if I remembered telling him to ask me if he needed help. I went into my pocket. I had a five, a ten, two singles. I took the ten and held it out. He looked at it horrified and pushed my hand back.

"No, no, man!" he said. "Just those!"

"Two bucks? You sure?"

"Yeah! Just till Thursday!"

For the next two days I didn't see him. Early on Thursday I had to go out to Jersey. I got back to Penn Station after three and caught a cab home. Coming down Lex, the cabbie waited for an Indian man to cross the street, then cut off his trailing wife to nudge the big Caprice around the corner. Down the street I saw Jimmy in front of my building. When the cab stopped, he came up to the door, then backed off and looked away while I paid for the ride. He looked so happy to see me I was scared his grin would bust his face. He proudly held out two bucks. He'd rolled them up like a handmade cigarette.

"You been waiting?" I said.

"Naw, not waiting, just in the neighborhood, you know?"

He kept moving back and forth, still eager, like things weren't settled all the way. I told him thanks. He told me I was welcome. I stood there holding the money. I didn't want to put it in my pocket in front of him.

"Aren't you gonna spend it?" he said. "Get yourself a beer or something?"

I caught on. He'd gone since Monday thinking that by borrowing it, he'd deprived me of spending it. The debt wouldn't be fully paid until I broke the thirst he'd imposed on me.

"Sure," I said. "Let's go."

He shook his head and shied away. "Naw. I don't drink. But I know you been waiting to have one."

We headed for the Bank Cafe on the far corner of Third, a new joint, all glass along the walls that faced the sidewalks. I went in and took a stool at the empty afternoon bar and ordered a Rolling Rock.

He stayed outside, patrolling back and forth along the windows, looking in every few seconds. I held the bottle up. His grin broke out. He waved and kept patrolling. Halfway through the bottle he was satisfied. He cupped his eyes and looked inside a final time, over the heads of a startled couple at a window table, grinned and waved again, then turned and crossed back over Third, his debt paid, his world right again, his overcoat sailing on the heat of that August afternoon.

I look at the London Cobra Show as arguably the best event of this hobby. Two to three hundred Cobras converge on an Ohio town for a long weekend of parades, autocrosses, cruises, barbecues. Our hobby's rational answer to Sturgis. But what gives it the heart that makes it my personal favorite are the charity burnout rides the guys give spectators — young and old alike — down Main Street. There's nothing like a Cobra. You can see it all over their faces. Zero to ninety in the fire and thunder and smoke of a couple of blocks. I always think of a hundred people I'd like to buy that ride for. My kids and grandkids. The niece and nephew who look to me as the closest thing to a dad. The young cheerful disabled guy who helps me pull cardboard out of my car at the local recycling place. People I'd like to mend long-broken fences with. And a street guy called Jimmy I last saw 25 years ago. I can't imagine that the trajectory of his life has altered much. He could easily still be there, on 30th Street, his dreads veined with silver, his grin tempered some by that relentlessly grim city, still keeping the neighborhood honest the way he did for me. A ride in a Cobra would scare him a million times more than a ten dollar bill. But man would I like to take that ten he wouldn't take and buy him one.

Chrome Blue

Steed's Texaco stood on the corner of Main Street and Third North in my home town of Bountiful. Back in high school, when Bobby West pumped gas and did brake jobs there, the double bay was where we sometimes hung out, working on our own cars. It was where we hung scavenger pipes under the locked rear axle of Zesiger's 40 Ford, tapped a wolf whistle into the manifold of Gardiner's 52 Olds, set razor blades into putty behind the hollow crossbars of Rasmussen's spinner hubcaps to keep them from being swiped again. It was where we solved the long mystery of the bad smell in Bobby's 57 Pontiac, a smell we never tracked down for the month it took to run its course, one we forgot about until the night we hoisted the Pontiac to put shackles in the front end, and found the mummified head of a cat stuck up on top of the frame behind the left front wheel, nothing left but skull and fur and a fixed expression of stark and silent terror. There was Derby who wanted to hang the head off the rearview mirror of his bugeye Sprite. Rasmussen and his hand-me-down old Rambler. Flowers and his smoking Renault Dauphin.

Baty and his mom's 59 Impala, whose brake lights we wired to the ruby eyes of a hula dancer with a pair of eyehooks for a pelvis, and then mounted on the turtledeck behind the back seat. All light bolt-on stuff at first, but as time went on, we got to doing deeper stuff. Breaking down and building up engines. Cracking open transmissions. Stuff none of us would have had the guts to try if it hadn't been for Bobby West.

He and I were about the same size. He was built a little tougher. He was better looking, had the edge on me on being smooth, paid a lot more attention to looking good. Most of the car guys then were greasers. Flamboyant pompadours, fenders, duck's ass haircuts. Not Bobby. He just kept his dark hair trimmed, trained, close to home. He had these incredible blue eyes shot through with chips of what looked like reflected chrome. All of us — Baty, Rasmussen, Flowers, Derby, Jensen, West — met and started hanging out when we were twelve, neighborhood and church buddies, bike riders, playing cards in the rear spokes, except for Bobby. Even back then, his license four years off, he maintained this quiet automotive vigilance, kept those blue eyes focused on the horizon where chrome glinted deep in the heart of some mirage. It wasn't arrogance that kept him off a bike. It was the haunting need to stay focused and not look away lest it disappear. When we hit sixteen, finally licensed, it was obvious that there was more to Bobby's vigilance than hunger. There was a gift. Over the next few years I would learn everything I knew about cars from him. What I would learn in particular was how to work on them. Start by knowing what you want and where you're going. Take one step at a time to get there. Never cut a corner. Never let yourself get scared. Keep things in order and things will always make sense.

Steed's Texaco was the schoolhouse. It was where we gathered to avail ourselves of a hoist, real tools, Bobby's quiet genius and nerve. It was where we assembled at pivotal times of our lives to move forward more or less together through our rites of passage. After hours, we'd bring in chairs from the office, raise a hoist to where we could use it as a bench, consider our lives in the smell of grease and gas and exhaust, the hammer of a compressor, the blast of an overhead heater, cans of Olympia in the old round-topped fridge, someone's car always there in the other bay, on the hoist, its wheels hanging. We graduated high school. We did the army. We came home, found girls, were best men at one another's weddings. Bobby was driving a 66 Malibu Supersport by then. I had a 67 GTO. Somewhere in there he got a vintage pickup. I picked up a Speedster. Both of them had seen their share of bondo, bad paint, rust, to where we decided to blast them clean. We stripped them down to shells — no trim, upholstery, glass, handles, lights — and on a Sunday set up shop with a rented sandblaster on the lot at Steed's Texaco. I went first. As always, I relied on Bobby not just for what to do, but for the nerve to do it. The angle to use. How close to keep the nozzle. How fast. What to look for to know you're not cutting too shallow or deep. While we were doing his pickup it started clouding over. We swept the place up under a gathering overcast and then hurried our illegal bare steel vehicles to his mom's house where we were planning to hit them with primer. It started sprinkling. Thunder rocketed overhead. He opened the door to the one spare stall in his mom's garage. Get the Porsche inside, he said. No, I said. Your truck. Forget the truck, he said. No, I said. It's your garage. That's right, he said. So move it. Inside, using a couple of rattlecans of red oxide, we primered the Speedster while his truck stood outside in a cloudburst, its steel skin taking on the same dull color. That was him. The kind of guy he was.

Bobby — along with Baty and Flowers and Jensen and the rest of the gang — would stay around Salt Lake and its outlying towns. Keep the faith. Build lives there. Buy houses. Stock them with kids. I would go the other way. It wasn't long before the distance between us — social, religious, cultural — felt too great to stay in touch. The last time I saw them was somewhere in my twenties. When I left to pick my life up elsewhere, the distance became geographical, and for the next few decades, time would lengthen it as well. I would conclude that those boyhood friendships had been meant to last only long enough to serve their purpose. They were over. I could replicate the Speedster. But Toni would only know that seminal part of my life in the stories I told her. I would only have those friendships back by writing those stories down. And then one of them found me.

Five of them still got together. They wanted to see me too. Last month Toni and I flew out to spend a week with them. I'd forgotten those chrome blue eyes. That purposeful attitude. He and Vicky had seen five kids through college and had a dynasty of grandkids. He still had his 66 Supersport. When he fired it up it ran with the same tight restless hunger it had when we used to drag State Street. It needed paint. He talked about stripping it. I thought back to sanding out the paint on my replica Speedster. Finding the nerve to do it — as I had for so many tasks that had seemed insurmountable — by remembering Bobby West. The pickup whose steel he sacrificed to the rain was gone. Steed's Texaco was gone. And now any distance between us — if there had ever been any — was history too.

The Second Coming

Harold Camping, now deceased, was a self-anointed prophet with a radio show who predicted that Christ would return to Earth on May 21, 2011, and the saved would be caught up in the clouds and meet the Lord in the air in what is called the rapture. That date came — and went — during the weekend of the Carlisle Nationals. This story is an eyewitness account of that apocalyptic event.

I'm not sure what the rapture is. What I understand is that some of your more righteous friends just suddenly disappear. Get yanked out of shoes they won't be needing again. Well, if that's how it happens, there are probably worse places to sit out the latest rapture — scheduled for the evening of Saturday May 21st — than the Carlisle Import and Replicar Nationals. First, you won't lose many of your friends, because at heart you're pretty much all garage savages, parts mongerers, tool junkies, obsessive compulsive polishers, hosts to some other heretical disorder that disqualifies you from being called. Second, the import crowd is there, Porsche and other guys delusional enough to think they'll be among the chosen, and it's bound to get interesting watching them run through what's left on their bucket lists. Especially the Peugeot and Citroen guys.

Saturday starts out as anything but the first day of the rest of the planet's life. It's beautiful, the sky clear, the sun taking the night rain off the air, a rare Carlisle day, the show field a dazzling festival of cars, coolers, lawn chairs. A live band kicks out Eagles tunes. At the food court guys wolf down Carlisle High School Marching Band egg sandwiches. Nothing contradicts the expectation that they'll be back tomorrow having another one. Spectators meander among cars with their cameras and sun hats and questions. Nothing suggests that in the morning only their shoes may still be here. Guys motor around the field in each other's projects. The rising howl of some car on the dyno rack periodically breaks an easy conversation. Nobody seems to care or remember what day it is. Nobody's watching CNN. I wander over to the Saab area with a question of my own.

"So this is the most intelligent car ever built, huh?"

He's a young guy whose nametag says he's Roy. He's standing next to a black 900 Turbo with the windows tinted deeper than my WileyX biker shades.

"So they say," he says, looking for my eyes.

"How do they know?"

"It's just something they say."

"Do they teach it things and give it tests?"

He looks harder for my eyes.

"Is it smarter than a Smart Car?" I say.

"Ha ha," he says.

"Japanese cars are pretty smart too," I say. "They're real serious about education."

"Then maybe you should go talk to them," he suggests.

"You ready for the rapture?"

"What's the rapture?" he says.

"Ask your car."

Things change over the afternoon. At first it's this restless feel to the air, like the day is losing patience with itself, tired of holding this pose of rare perfection, wanting to get back to being a Carlisle day. Clouds start sending long white feelers out across the sky. By three, the big ones are rolling in, the big biblical Cecil B. DeMille jobs, roiling with portent. It's then that we start hearing urgent whispers of the coming rapture. "It's supposed to happen at six," Linda says. "I heard eight," says Norma. "Nope," says Danny. "Midnight."

Around four, a menacing sprinkle starting, the Speedster and Spyder guys start leaving to get back to the hotel for the raffle before heading out to dinner at Sunnyside Restaurant. I tell them I'll hook up with them there. I want to stick around. See who disappears. Things are calm around our part of the field because kit and replica guys know that raptures don't apply to them. But things start getting hairy over on the import side. It looks like word's got out. They've got a fire barrel going. When I wander over, guys are throwing licenses, registrations, insurance cards, cash, keys, credit cards into its roaring heart. The Saab guy named Roy goes to toss his license in. "Are you nuts?" I tell him. He gives me this stark blind crazy look. "I'll never need this crap again!" he hollers. "I'm outta here!"

Things fall apart, writes Yeats, in his poem "The Second Coming." The center cannot hold. The Volvo guys, sick to death of safety, start a demolition derby, setting off airbags, smoking their Onstars, alarms squealing like a chorus of stuck pigs. The Peugeot and Citroen guys are lined up at the dyno rack, hungry to blow up engines they've had to baby for years like nasty chihuahuas. The British guys are clipping their Lucas systems to a 220 volt extension line, standing back, cackling their arses off while wires sizzle and smoke like sparklers and lights and gauges and horns explode. The Audi, Benz, and Bimmer guys are having a leather eating contest, seeing who can put away their interior the fastest. The Saab guys are looking for third graders to test their cars against. The Porsche guys — it's time to head for Sunnyside.

After dinner, from the restaurant parking lot, the overcast glows red above the show field, a familiar fire deep inside its belly. Back at the hotel we hunker down for a night of drinking in the hospitality suite. By midnight we're down to a hardcore few around a conference table. For the last hour, mild-mannered Hoss Hallstrand has been sitting there in quiet contemplation, immune to all the rowdy talk around him. All of a sudden he's doing Flip Wilson's Geraldine. I mean really doing her. Outraged. Righteous. Implacable. Lane Anderson morphs into this whiskey-voiced radio guy from Charleston and starts announcing a WWF bout. And then Toni gets taken over by Lucille, the long-retired Vegas showgirl who lives in an Airstream outside Barstow, and Lucille is all Geraldine needs. They go at each other like they're on The Maury Show. For a while there, until Hoss and Lane and Toni make it back, we've got our rapture.

Sunday morning, given the cloud-borne fire we saw last night, I expect the show field to be scorched. It isn't. Just some bashed Volvos, some Peugeots and Citroens with their hoods shredded and the rubble of their engines scattered around the dyno rack, German sedans with their leather interiors ripped out, TR4s with burn scars where their wires ran, a sheepish bunch of stupid-looking Saabs. I look for the guys who own them to see who disappeared. They're all there, soaked from another rain, huddled in the mud, wrapped in car covers like kids in Woodstock blankets, unlicensed, unregistered, uninsured, broke. The Saab guy asks for a buck for breakfast. I look away from the devastation of this failed rapture out toward the calm center of the field. What I see stops me cold. There it stands, by itself again, on a clearing of lush grass. Four years ago, looking to do our own version of the Burning Man festival, we lifted it ten stories high into the sunset, piled Duraflame logs around the shaft of the swaying hoist, watched the flames rise and start licking at its undercarriage. I know why last night's fire looked familiar. New, sparkling, unscathed, but still unmistakable, there it is again, the little red Fiero we torched in a mock sacrifice to the donor gods, back among us. I missed the chance to interview it then. I head across the grass.

The Onion Eater

Back in college I worked one Christmas break at one of the grand old railroad depots in Salt Lake — I can't remember whether it was the Rio Grande or Union Pacific — pulling mail bags full of Christmas cards and presents out of boxcars. There was a bulletin board in the break room. Someone had tacked up a newspaper article about the discovery of a hormone that reduced cholesterol. The hormone was triggered and released, the article said, by one of two activities: eating raw onions or making love. I'd heard my mom fret my dad to death about watching his cholesterol. I figured he might find the information useful. That night, when he picked me up on his own way home from work, I told him about the article. I knew enough about making love back then to know that it was anything but compatible with eating onions raw. They were about as diametrically opposed and mutually repulsive as you could get. Unless your partner wore nose plugs, or ate an onion too, you had to choose. The choice to me seemed like a no-brainer. Riding home, snow in the headlights, I mentioned that to my dad too. That you couldn't do both. That you had to choose.

"Then I'll have to stop and get some onions," he said.

He wasn't laughing. Not even smiling. The resignation in his voice made my blood run cold. In the dim light from the dashboard his face looked grave. I looked ahead again, out the windshield, where the storm was picking up, the headlights setting fire to spiraling pinpoints of snow rushing out of the dark at us. He may have been in his late forties then. He didn't seem old. He was a younger man than I am now. I'd never known why an onion could make a man cry. That night it made sense.

Starting in 2000, and going for several years, I wrote the monthly newsletter for the New Jersey Replicar Club. The other night I came across some issues and made the mistake of rifling through them. Toni was out at one or another meeting. I don't know why I started reading. The club has been disbanded for two or three years. This was the time of year we'd be in full swing, one activity after another, and it could have been just the yearning to see those folks again. I let myself get lost in stories going back ten years on Carlisle, on Memorial Motor Madness in the M&M plant parking lot in Hackettstown, on the Fourth of July Parade in Randolph. Cruise nights. Impromptu rallies up into the hills of the Poconos and out along the Delaware River. Saturdays in someone's garage. The annual club picnic on a lazy lakeside Saturday afternoon in August. The Solberg and Shawnee Balloon Festivals. The Southern Adventure. The Popcorn Run through the fiery October foliage of northwest Jersey. The annual winter banquet. The meetings once a month. I remember pulling into the parking lot of Harry's business off Montesano Road when I first joined. In the lot, in the faint light of the high overhead lamp, there would be six, seven, maybe eight of the guys, cigarette smoke rising, Tommy's MG, Rocky's Speedster, Jerry's Sebring, Dick's Ferrari Boxer, Tim's Grand Sport, Warren's GT40, Bob's Cobra among the cars sometimes lined up across the lot. Hands came out of the dark. I shook them. Except for the meetings there were always women. Always. Wives and girlfriends. On the road to Carlisle, at the M&M plant, for the rallies and runs, the picnics and festivals, holding that right seat and sometimes the driver's seat down. What the meetings made clear was the sobering contrast between life with them and life without them. With them we were whole. There was symmetry. Without them we were a pretty sad gang of clueless old guys with empty right seats and onion breath. One of the newsletters told the story of the last time Toni and I did the Randolph Parade in the Speedster. A couple of guys from a hillside whistled when we passed. I gave them a thumbs up. "Yeah," one of them yelled, "the car's nice too."

Back in the sixties Henry Mancini wrote a song called "Two for the Road" that serves as the theme to a movie of the same name starring Audrey Hepburn and Albert Finney. They first meet when she's in a touring girl's choir and he's a struggling young architect. The movie shifts back and forth in time to chronicle maybe twenty years of their life together through the usual milestones of any couple's journey: courtship, marriage, career, infidelity, parenthood, success. Pretty much all the scenes, in one way or another, are road scenes. The milestones are marked by the sequence of cars they go through: an MG TD, a Triumph Herald, a VW Microbus, a Ford Country Squire, and a Mercedes Benz 230 SL. I don't know if the "Our Song" tradition is still in practice these days. But "Two for the Road" is the song Toni and I chose two decades ago when we didn't know what the road was or where it would lead. In 1999 it led to a

Speedster replica, which led to the NJRC, which led to where we are now, where most of our active friends and acquaintances come from the world of this hobby. They are impossible to separate from their cars. John and Marian and their Diva. Sandy and Dave and their Cobra. Norma and Bruce and their Speedster. All of us know the story. "Two for the Road" is a beautiful ballad that I think embodies the shamelessly romantic heart of that story. Bruce and Julie from Ohio. Jack and Alice from Arkansas. The Strouds clear from Ottawa. All of us.

There are things you never want your dad to tell you. That he had to choose raw onions over making love is one of them. Riding home with him that night, I remember looking out the windshield, promising myself that if I ever heard that much resignation in my own voice, I'd kill myself. I never actually saw him eat an onion. He favored baloney and veal loaf. Cholesterol, despite my mother's constant nattering, was never a problem. He lived to see ninety. He died with his heart strong and his arteries clean. But there are things your mom or dad can casually say that will stay with you for life. Once, to see what it would be like if my life turned out celibate, I ate one. It wasn't bad. If you held your breath it had the taste and texture of some Caribbean breed of apple.

I've lived long enough to have learned that there's the rare occasion where a raw onion may be what you're left with. Where "One for the Road" or "Hit the Road Jack" is a more appropriate song choice. Fine. No problem. Fire up the Speedster. Head for the next town west of here. Stop at the supermarket and buy a single onion. No, I tell the cashier, I don't need a bag. By the time I get back to the Speedster, it's peeled, and I'm biting into raw fruit, and my eyes are watering, and my breath is a flamethrower that backs all the gathered tourists off, chases away the sweet young thing who had the temerity to think she could actually get in and occupy the seat I always keep reserved for Toni.

Actual Miles

Ray Carver was a writer whose career began in the Northwest in the early sixties, steadily and quietly built an under-the-radar following across the country, and continued into the eighties when he was "discovered" by the East Coast literati and *The New Yorker* magazine. He was arguably the most influential American short story writer of the last century. He wrote about ordinary people confronted with ordinary events. Fishing. Drinking. Looking for work. Breaking up. Not knowing how to get rid of a vacuum cleaner salesman. Setting all the furniture out for a yard sale, arranging it the way it was when it was in the house, and running extension cords so people could turn on lamps, play the stereo, dance. Or just a haircut. He knew there was something there that was extraordinary. And he always found it.

The heading for the column I wrote for *Kit Car Builder*, and the title of this book, "Actual Mileage," comes from a story of his called "Are These Actual Miles?" Quickly told, a typical Carver couple has squandered what money they had, gone broke, maxed out their cards, and need to sell their Lincoln convertible to stay off the street. The husband gets the Lincoln ready. His wife cleans herself up and goes out and starts hitting used car dealers. He stays home. She calls to tell him she found a buyer and they're going out for a drink to seal the deal. She calls later to say they're having dinner. Later still to tell him they're having drinks again. Anyway, she doesn't show up till morning, tousled, puffy, sleepless. The husband's been up all night, drinking and waiting, working himself up, and when she comes in, he runs outside for a showdown. The guy, a used car salesman, is backing the Lincoln out of the driveway. He stops. There's the threat of a fight but they come to a tacit understanding that none of it is worth it. Ray's characters always knew that some macho Hemingway fistfight never solved anything. The salesman starts backing out again, then pulls forward, rolls down the window. "Just between you and me," he asks the husband, "are these actual miles?"

I've always liked his work because it's about people like me, who come from the places I do, who live around the edges the way I have, often unable to get out of their own way. Hey. That's me. I bought a Kirby vacuum from that guy. And I've always liked the story about the Lincoln because I have similar ones. A waitress and an old Corvair. A cowgirl and a 65 Pontiac Catalina. A receptionist and a 72 Dodge Dart. A surgical assistant and a 53 Roadmaster Riviera. A rat 2002 and a redheaded hippie with an Irish Setter, and yeah, Hoss, it had a red bandana for a neckerchief. But you get the gist. Behind every car worth remembering is someone or something you'd probably rather forget. I'm sure you've got stories of your own. Or you can read Ray's.

I also like the Lincoln story, of course, because it's a car story. Ray had a drinking problem he managed to beat the last few successful and happy years of his life. I don't know what he knew about cars, but from a story I heard, he knew that a car with four flat tires could get you to the liquor store and back, and maybe that was where his automotive know-how began and ended. Unlike me, Ray never had the good fortune to write for a magazine about building cars, and I've sometimes wondered what kind of story he'd write about a guy who wanted to build one. He died in 1988 of cancer at the age of 50, and so it's probably sacrilegious to take a stab at what he'd do, but it may go like this. Let's call the guy Bill. The kit Bill would want to build wouldn't be a mainstream kit like a Cobra or Speedster or Lambo or MG or street rod. In keeping with characters who can't get out of their own way, he'd want something offbeat that would doom him from the start, some one-of-a-kind contraption with a provenance not even Harold Pace could track down. It wouldn't be a Brubaker Box, or a Bradley, or a Valkyrie, but it would combine design features from all three, something Ray would leave to you to visualize. He might call it a Raptor. Living in an apartment with only street parking, Bill would get permission from his ex to have it delivered to the house he used to share with her and her no-load son, and put it on cinderblocks in the dirt outside the master bedroom window. Bill wouldn't have known that it came without wheels and a chassis. So, after retreating into drinking for a week to come to a solution, he would strip the body and bed off an old Datsun pickup. Then, discovering that nothing fit up, he'd spend another week drunk, sober up and start mounting the body to the frame with cargo straps and duct tape. In the meantime his ex would have started a thing with the guy who delivered it. He'd be an amiable guy named Ted. Over time, Ted and Bill would strike up a friendship, start drinking together, lounging out in the bucket seats

Bill was storing in his living room. Bill would start on the wiring. Ted would ignore Bill's ex to help him. They would run an extension cord from the master bedroom to test things as they went. The horn button would set the brakelights off. The left turn signal would blow out the right front tire. The ignition switch would start the swamp cooler. After drinking for another week, Bill and Ted would make the decision to spend the winter in rehab, and the no-load son and his girlfriend would paint all the windows black and turn the Raptor into a pot den.

For those of you who majored in something more compensatory than English, there's an old convention from the days of Greek theater called "deus ex machina," which translates to "god from a machine." The "machine" refers to a mechanical device — a crane or lift — that would introduce an actor playing one or another god onto the stage. The god would resolve the snarled plot and end the play. These days it's viewed as a copout. An overambitious writer works himself deep into the jungle of a tangled plot and can't find his way home. So he introduces some improbable contrivance to end things. A winning lottery ticket. A ray of Mary Poppins sunshine. The worst of them will simply kill off the character. Lightning, a speeding train, a bullet that made it all the way from Omaha to Corvallis. This is where I find myself. I'm not Ray Carver. I'm not that good. Where he could take what I've thrown together and bring it to a place of illumination, this place of quiet insight into human frailty, I can't. I have to do the deus ex machina thing. And so I call the closest thing to a god I know in this situation. The Car Whisperer. "Alan. It's Max." "Hey buddy. What's up?" "I found this kit you need to help me rescue." "Yeah? What you got?" "It's a Raptor." "Oh. Sure. I've done a couple of those."

2012

Stealing Thunder

Once a month or so I'll cruise the websites of some of our Cobra clubs. Arizona Cobras, the Tennessee and Kentucky clubs, the Great Lakes guys, the Australian and Canadian sites, the London Cobra Show. Take video strolls through 200 tethered Cobras waiting to race or cruise. The sense of assembled power is rousing and unforgettable. I take my latest cruise one Sunday morning a month ago. Watch clips of the London guys doing burnout runs down Main Street. That afternoon we visit Dave and Sandy. Dave owns this awesome Unique Cobra 427 named Thunder and painted this deep rich flawless maroon. He's probably the most meticulous and proud and committed Cobra guy I know. Let me add paranoid — in a protective way — to that mix. He's raced it a couple of times on the road course at Pocono. At Carlisle you'll see him tirelessly answer people's questions. His wife Sandy has this fresh and easy laugh and wears this quietly solicitous Mona Lisa smile when it comes to the object of Dave's obsession. I'm still on a power high from the morning's virtual cruise through Cobra Country. At Dave and Sandy's

house, I can't stop excusing myself, heading out to the most immaculate garage I've ever seen, looking Thunder over, where Dave
keeps finding me.

"So do you have any questions?"

I haven't kept count. It could be anywhere from the seventeenth
to the fortieth time he's found me out here.

"Yeah. But I'd just forget the answers."

"Oh, for Pete's sake, then," he finally says. "Just take Toni and
go for a ride."

It's October and in the seventies and the foliage has just peaked.
I'm shy at first. I'm riding something exponentially more serious
than a little fourbanger Speedster. The whole car trembles with
torque and horsepower it's restless to use. Filtered sunlight ripples
across Toni's face. I keep to back roads to get used to this much har-
nessed hairtrigger lunacy. Eventually we're on Route 206, headed
through Sussex County toward the Pennsylvania border, and it's
somewhere along there that one of us — I'm not sure who — comes
up with the bright idea of stealing it.

That's actually a lie. It's me. My idea. My mouth it comes out of.

"Steal it?" says Toni.

"Yeah."

"You mean really steal it. Like in not take it back."

"I always wanted one," I tell her. "I got me one."

"Dave's your friend."

"Sandy can calm him down."

"You forget," Toni says. "There's no such word as calm when it
comes to Dave and his car."

I keep Thunder headed northwest up Route 206. We're through
Montague, coming down the hill to the toll bridge across the Dela-

ware that takes us into Pennsylvania.

"You're going across?" she says.

"Yeah."

"You're really doing this. Stealing his car."

"Yeah."

"I'm calling someone."

I reach across, grab her crackberry, toss it over my head. In the rearview mirror I watch it hit the pavement in this skittering explosion of keys the size of ladybugs. Toni gets the message too. That I've turned into someone neither one of us can recognize.

"Where are we going?" she says.

Where do you go in a stolen Cobra? Good question. But I've already got an answer. There's a show on the History Channel called IRT Deadliest Roads. It's a spin-off of Ice Road Truckers — hence the IRT — to the degree that it even uses the same drivers. Instead of Alaska and Canada, though, it tackles the Andes of Bolivia and Peru. And you're not riding in Petes and Kenworths. Rickety old leaky Volvo dumptrucks are used to haul loads to remote villages deep in the Andes along roads that are long crumbling notches cut into the vertical sides of mile high cliffs. My favorite is one that goes up a mountain range in so many twisted switchbacks it looks like someone laid a line of silly string back and forth across its face. I don't know where to look for switchbacks in the eastern United States. But I remember some pretty good stretches in the Rockies. Alpine Loop up the Timpanogos Range. The Sierras out of Reno. And there used to be some good ones coming off Cabbage Hill out of the Blue Mountains.

"Idaho," I tell her, remembering that's how you get into the Blues from here. I shoot the Cobra through an E-ZPass booth. Dave can field the ticket. At least he'll have another photo of his car. Going through Milford Toni's looking for an opportunity to jump. The minute I slow to walking speed, she'll bail, so I've got to time the lights to keep Thunder rolling. Thunder rolling, I think. Rolling Thunder. Pretty cool. And then I can't stop laughing.

"Please tell me you're not doing this," she says. "Please tell me we're going back."

"To what?"

"To Dave and Sandy's. Then home."

Soon we're through Milford. Heading up toward Interstate 84. From 84 we catch 81 and then 80 West from there. The sun's ahead of us, but toward the south this time of year, when the air loses its capacity to hold heat. It isn't long before we're rolling through the dark and cold and isolation of the Pennsylvania night.

"Honey," she says, from next to me. "I'm hungry and cold."

"I know."

Where we are. How far we've come. How many times we've stopped just for gas. How many days. It comes to where I don't know. This much wind. This much dark. This much noise this long. I can't remember when I started losing it. I have to keep looking over at Toni, huddled and shivering, to keep her from turning into the rocking mummy of Mrs. Bates in Psycho. In the blaze of oncoming headlights my lips and eyelids and scalp feel like they're gone. So this is what it's like, I'm finally thinking, stealing your friend's car. When it comes to Dave it's a crime that's most likely irreversible. When it comes to his Cobra it's stealing a 525 horsepower Picasso. We can't just turn around, drive back, show up at his house at sunrise with an apology. This will take some real long distance diplomacy. At a gas station with an actual pay phone I make the call.

"Sandy. It's Max. Dave there?"

"Max? Thank god! Dave's in Newton Memorial. He's under observation."

I start to whimper, like a kid, when I would break something only a grownup could fix.

"Someone stole Thunder," I tell her. "We stopped for a Coke and came out and it was gone. We just got it back."

"Stole it? Are you serious? Is it okay? Where are you?"

"Yeah. It's fine. Runs perfect. Not a scratch. We had to chase 'em into Iowa to catch 'em. We're on our way back now."

"Chase them how? Your car's here."

"Uhh . . . yeah. Hold on, Sandy . . . Toni?"

The Greatest Gig

We're standing around the fire barrel, Eddie and Robbie and me, burning the last of the bicycle tires Tommy found in a fleamarket booth, and we're talking about drinking milk and smoking cigarettes. It comes up because Eddie read this study in some newspaper that said milk was what caused lung cancer down in Argentina. Robbie says no. It's cigarettes. They just didn't look at the results the way they should have. See, he says, everyone in Argentina smokes from the time they're three years old, but not everyone drinks milk. Milk makes mucus. And mucus in your lungs is like glue for all the nasty stuff in smoke. If you don't drink milk, says Robbie, most all of that stuff gets blown back out without hurting anything. It doesn't stay stuck where it can do its dirty work. So it's still cigarettes that cause lung cancer. It's just that in Argentina, the milk drinkers are the ones who get it, and that's how milk gets blamed.

"See," he says, "up here, more people drink milk than smoke. So they know it ain't milk. Just from that."

"What about beer?" Eddie wants to know. "Does it make mucus?"

"All beer makes is pee," says Robbie. "What do you care, anyway? You don't smoke."

Standing there, holding my hands in the heat of the tire smoke, I'm suddenly thinking how long I've been doing this.

"Six years."

"Six years what?"

"Doing this page," I say. "Making stuff up. Like us being here."

We're here because we got hired this winter, Robbie and Eddie and Tommy and me, to be night watchmen for Carlisle. Through the smoke I'm looking at Robbie's and Eddie's faces in the red glow coming off the tires down inside the barrel. Off in the dark somewhere I can hear the golf cart Tommy's out there driving, checking the perimeter, looking for other stuff we can burn. Now and then I can hear him wind it out to cut some donuts on the frozen grass. I can tell you we're not the world's greatest sentries. It would make more sense to stand with our backs to the barrel, protect our night vision, keep a lookout. But this is Carlisle, it's January, and about the only things worth stealing are the urinals. Behind us, in the starlight, the bleachers rise up like the white ghost of a capsized hospital ship.

"Six years already," says Eddie.

"Yeah. Six a year. This one makes thirty-six."

"Maybe we oughta celebrate," Eddie says.

"You don't celebrate six years," says Robbie. "That's nowhere. Five, maybe. Then ten."

"I wasn't paying attention," I say.

"Six years," says Eddie. "I've never done anything that long."

"You ever get hate mail?" says Robbie.

"We could still celebrate," says Eddie.

Beginning with that initial column six years ago, about the way Rocky and I used to pimp our Speedsters to get into wine and music festivals for free, Boss Jim has always held me to the fenceline of this single page. I've only broken out once, to a page in the forties, for a paragraph or two before he found me. Beyond that, within this page, I've had the freedom to do most anything I've wanted. If my watchman buddies want to celebrate six years, well, we can do that. In a heartbeat I can have us all in Disneyland, the Bahamas, Hawaii. A sentence can put us in a penthouse suite at the Bellagio. Another sentence can have us eating chocolate dipped strawberries, sipping Cristal, the personal talents of a dozen plumed showgirls at our disposal. For that matter, I can make them rock stars, Eddie and Tommy and Robbie, and they won't need me to score women or anything else for them. As long as I stay on this page, the way I always have except for that one brief breakout, I can do what I want. I can call Mount Rushmore and rent the head of Abraham Lincoln for a party. Take a chartered jet from this field we're guarding straight to Rome to do shots of Jaegermeister with the Pope. And this is where Jim always taps me on the shoulder to remind me of Rule Two. Always make sure there's something automotive in the mix. Okay. No problem. Here, Eddie, the keys to that Regal Thunder over there. Robbie, you're a Ford guy too, so the plates on that Factory Five have your name on them. And here. Visa cards, hotel reservations, passes for the SEMA show. Now get going. It's a long drive. And take notes.

"Tommy. That Speedster's yours."

"A Speedster? How come they got —"

"I can always give you a burro. Wanna tour the Grand Canyon instead?"

"No. I'm good."

I can move the jet stream all the way up to the Arctic Circle and put the weather in the sunny seventies all the way across the northern United States and well up into Canada. I can give everyone who reads this page a GPS and a lifetime supply of gas. I can keep it from raining here in Carlisle the third weekend in May. And here's where Jim taps me on the shoulder with another rule. Don't touch the weather. Even though he doesn't say why, I take him serious, because there's some emotional scar tissue in the way he says it. But I could cure lung cancer in Argentina. I could invent milk that nothing sticks to and cigarettes that generate testosterone instead of tumor cells. I could have Jim give me a million dollar raise for what I do here on this page. And that's where he always stops me with another rule. You have to do ten years to get a raise. Not six. Not five. Ten. You know that.

So here we are, Eddie and Robbie and Tommy and me, guarding Carlisle so that when you guys show up in May you'll have urinals, and it's three in the morning and seven degrees in the shade, and I can't even make my own feet warm, can't even afford a six-pack celebration. Tommy comes back from foraging. He's got the cart loaded with tons of weathered old discarded goodie bags. They oughta burn well. Especially the aerosol cans of tire shine.

"See anyone out there?" says Robbie.

"Just those loser Speedster guys," says Tommy. "Camped at the main gate."

"Man," says Eddie. "They show up sooner every year."

Robbie's right about this anniversary. Six years is lame. In marital parlance it's probably the milk anniversary. It's something I should have done at the five year mark, a year ago, things I should have sat back and thought about and then said, but didn't remember to. So I'll say them now. Thanks to Carolyn for her forbearance in letting Actual Mileage occupy this page of her magazine for the last six years. Thanks to Jim for giving me the room to horse around and for having my back when the random piece of hate mail breaks the horizon. And thanks to you for what is still, six years later, the greatest gig I've ever had.

Jailbait

A neighbor friend of mine has a son I'll call Jed who's always loved my car. Twelve years ago, when it first showed up, he was there, a tow-headed kid I didn't know from down the road, watching it come off the truck. He loved having his picture taken in the driver's seat. Every few months he'd ask for a new one. Those photos chronicle his growth like the pencil marks of a kid's height on a kitchen wall. The car remains pretty much the same from one photo to the next. The setting is always the driveway. Jed is the one variable — the one thing that changes when you rifle through the photos. There was his long hair at twelve. There was his buzz cut a year or so later. There was his first moustache. There was an assortment of baseball caps. There was a high school graduation photo in his mortarboard and gown. As the photos progress you can see his face lean out, his shoulders fill more and more of the seat, his head rise higher above the backrest into the frame of the roll hoop, his big disarming California grin lose its babyfat vulnerability and grow more self-assured and measured. Sometimes he'd bring a buddy or two along, or a girlfriend, but if they wanted a shot of themselves in the car, they'd have to take a separate one. Jed always wanted to be photographed alone. I figured he wanted it that way so that when he showed anyone who was interested, it was like the car was his and his alone, a kid and his ride, ready for America. He always called it the Porsche. My friend wants to see the Porsche, he'd say, and ask if he could show him.

For high school he went to Sussex County Votech where he studied carpentry and started to hang out with car guys his own age. While he was there he salvaged, patched together, primered, and got a tired old 300Z running. It wasn't long before he was on a first name basis with every cop in the area. He was always a good-natured catch. If they got him for speeding, well, like any pick-up game, it was their job to score on him. No hard feelings. After Votech he couldn't find work as a carpenter. He moved to Newton, a neighboring town, took a job at a Pizza Hut, and got into the marijuana trade. He'd ride his bike to whatever alcove he used as his distribution point, let the air out of his back tire, tuck his nickel and dime and other bags inside, and make his rounds from there on foot. At the end of his day he'd pump his tire back up and head for home or work. It wasn't long before they caught him. I think they sentenced him to one day less than a year to keep from having to send him from county jail to Rahway State.

It was at his trial for heresy that Socrates said that the unexamined life is not worth living. For car guys like us, American misfits, you could just as easily say that a life without at least one arrest doesn't count for much either. Getting drunk on hard cider and running around the campus of the University of Utah naked. Pulling a guy through the driver's window at a stoplight on State Street to beat on his face. Doing 80 side by side past a children's hospital. Raiding a girls' dorm at Brigham Young University as the final stage of a rally with the ratty sports car gang you run with. Every time I've avoided jail can be attributed to one of three reasons. The cop was benevolent. The cop was negligent. I was too much of a stupid inconsequential little twerp to bring in. Sometimes, the way I'd get thrown back, I felt like a fish too small to legally keep.

Jed had an astonishing knack for taking things in stride. And I've never seen anyone who could make friends so easily and instantaneously. Jail? Okay. He didn't think orange was his color. But once he settled in, it was just another way to live, another kind of neighborhood, another set of stuff to do, another circle of friends, another place to make the Mark of Jed. Part of that mark, like it had always been, was the Porsche. One day I got a collect call. I knew it was him because there in the caller ID was the word correctional. Him saying his name in the blank space in the recording asking if I'd accept the charges. Good behavior had him down to less than seven weeks.

"I wanted to ask a favor," he said, after that and other catch-up stuff.

"What's that?"

"I really hope you're gonna say yes."

Hearing that disarming grin again, I couldn't help from smiling myself, knowing it was going to be impossible to say anything else.

"I gotta know what it is first."

"I told my friends here about the Porsche. I even showed 'em pictures I had my dad bring in."

"What'd they think?"

"They're like that's a crazy car. But half of 'em don't believe me and the other half wanna see it."

"Yeah?"

"So I was wondering if you could drive it over and park it on the roof of the garage. Just for a minute. So they'll know I ain't lying."

"The courthouse garage?"

"Yeah. We'll all be on the second floor. Not the courthouse. The jail."

"How do I know what's the second floor?"

"Just look for the window that's full of orange. I'll have every-body at one window. Why? You gonna do it?"

"You're not gonna tell 'em where I live, are you?"

"Man. I'm not stupid."

The kid I'm talking to is wearing orange for selling bags of weed out of the flat back tire of his bike.

"When do you want me there?"

It rains for the next week. He calls the first clear morning. In the meantime they've made him a trustee and moved him to the trustee block on the third floor. I should still look for the orange window. I tell him I'll be there at one.

I drive to Newton where the monolithic complex housing the courthouse and the jail stands. It's a cloudless day. Perfect car show weather. But this is a new kind of car show. I make a left at the end of Main up a hill whose vintage houses are occupied by law firms. Pull into the complex. A cop nods at me. A hangdog looking woman leaving court pulls hard on a cigarette. I drive up the dark ramps un-til I come out in daylight on the roof. I stop when I can see the big wall of the jail, several stories high, and start checking the massive windows. They're all black. Then, through the tint of the glass and the reflected silver of the sky, I can make out orange in one of them. And then arms waving. And then faces. Kids doing time for doing things I must have done myself. Too far away to tell which one is Jed. I do a couple of laps around the roof, park the Speedster angled toward them, get out and walk away. I know how this goes. They don't want to know the guy who drives it. They just want to see themselves the way Jed always did.

First Impression

Okay. Carlisle. My kid brother Marv shows up from Utah Wednesday for a two-week visit. He's been a jazz and blues musician all his life, knows about six instruments, has played in all kinds of bands. It's a life I envy and admire — the kind of life I might have had if I'd had his discipline. We spend Thursday getting the Speedster ready for its first Carlisle appearance in maybe five years. It doesn't go well. At the local motor vehicle office, looking to renew the registration, we're told that my plates are illegal. A new law, enacted two years ago when I wasn't paying attention, says that I have to run historic plates, and I'll need to jump through a week of burning hoops to get them. Back home, we try to get the engine lid back on, and waste two hours trying to figure out how to line these hot new hinges up.

By now, between illegal plates, a 2007 inspection sticker, and no engine lid, I start to make the usual excuses for leaving the thing home. Between a houseful of granddaughters here for Mothers' Day weekend, meeting a deadline for some procedures for a power plant in Anchorage, and putting the first book of my trilogy up on Amazon and Barnes & Noble, I'm whipped anyway. I start down that slippery path of thinking that maybe my Carlisle friends will let me get away with showing up in the Audi one more year. But then Danny and Lenny came down two Saturdays ago — Danny from Wallkill and Lenny all the way from Bristol — to work a nasty miss out of the engine. So there went that excuse. And the new excuses turn to dust when I hold them to the light. Illegal plates and an inspection sticker five years past its expiration date? Well, not that much of the ride will be in Jersey, so we only have to dodge cops till we clear the Delaware. No engine lid? Who needs one? The forecast is for Arizona weather all the way through Sunday. Besides, with the engine exposed, the road gawkers riding in the blind spot off my shoulder will have more stuff to take phone pictures of.

And there's my brother Marv. He's heard about this field of dreams called Carlisle now for years. Did he come all the way from Utah to watch his hangdog older brother let down his friends again by showing up in the Audi one more pathetic time? No. He's here to be impressed the way he impresses me, to take pride in this guy he's always tried to look up to, the way he did when I told him that Rocky owned the Susquehanna River and Alan built the Verrazano Bridge all by himself. So on Friday morning it's the Speedster that comes out of the garage, shaking five years of stiffness out of its joints, rubbing sleep out of its headlights. And if we're leaving the engine lid home, hell, we may as well leave the top home too, along with the sunblock I'm too clueless to think of. Marv rides shotgun in a baseball cap and a starter tan from playing golf since March. Me, I'm white as a basement spider, oblivious enough to go hatless under a clear sky and a hundred sixty miles of unforgiving sun. Toni falls in behind us in her S2000.

Some of the folks in the club make their pilgrimage to Carlisle from as far away as Arkansas and Michigan and Florida. Dave and Fran Stroud made the ride down from Ottawa. Not satisfied, apparently, with that quick a ride, they drove cross country down to Key West before coming north to Carlisle to make the trip worthwhile, and guarantee themselves the coveted "longest distance driven" award. Other guys just drive their Speedsters all the time. Cory Drake made his clamshell job the only car he owns. MusbJim's is coming up on eighty or ninety thousand miles. I don't know why I let my Speedster sit that long. Maybe because it didn't have a squeaky wheel that was crying to be greased. Other stuff insisted on coming first. I was writing the first two books of a trilogy, working with agents and publishers, helping Toni keep our business going. Somewhere in there that lunatic bare-toothed passion — that "madness" when all that mattered was building and getting my Speedster on the road — began to slip away. The sense of what it was like to put on some Santana, head west, and get lost in the rolling farms and foothills of the Delaware Basin and the Poconos just gradually faded. And then the engine developed that nasty way of stuttering, backfiring, cutting out, and my mechanic was too overworked to return my calls, and everything finally got easier to ignore than deal with, and then, on a day I couldn't name, its long sleep started. Over time it became a source less of pleasure than of guilt. And then guilt bred resentment. And then it became something to avoid. Jed still brought his friends to look at it. I'd pull its tonneau back to show them the interior. But through their excitement I could catch them taking a look at the dust — this haze of brown velvet — like mold on its silver paint.

I met Danny Piperato back in 2001 soon after I first had the Speedster on the road. Rocky and Linda and Toni and I drove up to a park outside Montgomery, New York, for the Tri-State VW Show. The rolling fields of grass were covered with beetles and buses in all their eccentric deadhead splendor. We were put in a class with other VW-based cars. I scored my first trophy — a people's choice for first in class. It was close to time to go when this animated guy with a boyish face and a blond crewcut was suddenly there. He was all over the Speedster. He wanted to talk. He wanted to know things I couldn't tell him. A new Vintage Spyder kit — not a roller but an actual kit — was still crated in his garage. He was getting ready to build it. He was aligning his life in a way that would let him build it. On the dirt path behind us a VW — maybe a Jetta — stood waiting. It wasn't a show car. Just a family car. Two little kids watched from its back seat. In the passenger seat was a woman. Her vibe wasn't what you'd call car friendly. I felt my Speedster wince. Danny and I talked for maybe fifteen minutes before she put the needle in her doll that made him turn around and leave. I liked him. And figured I'd probably never see him again. When I did, at Carlisle maybe five years later, he had to re-introduce himself.

The rest is history. The way he kept after me. Came down not once but three times, with parts, to help me get the Speedster running. Kept faith in something I'd relinquished. On the way to Carlisle, at the wheel, the backs of my hands turning this bright irreversible red, it came back. It had never gone too far. We got to Carlisle where Danny's open friendship and eager generosity was multiplied a hundred times. Tom Buchanan secretly installing a tunnel-mounted cupholder and basket in my car. A crew replacing a toasted set of wheel bearings in a crippled Speedster. People treating my kid brother Marv like they'd known him as long and well as they'd known me. Over and over. That was what got to him. I was glad to have my Speedster there. Glad to be back among the living.

Headed West

"You got it mapped out?"

"Yep. Columbus the first night. St. Louis the second. Then Oklahoma City. Then Albuquerque. The rest of the way on Friday."

He's telling us how he's making the ride from Jersey to Arizona to start his job teaching health and physical education at an elementary school in Mesa. He's driving his four-year-old Hyundai Accent. I'm guessing, but from the stops he's named, he'll be taking 80 across Pennsylvania into Ohio, doing a stretch on 70, dropping southwest on 71 to pick up 70, dropping southwest again on 44 to pick up 40 and ride it the rest of the way out west.

"Got rooms lined up?"

"Yep. They've all got free wifi too."

"So you'll be there Friday," his mom says.

"Yep." He glances away and then back. He heard it too, the hitch, the way her voice went high just for an instant. "That's when I sign the lease."

I've held her hand for a week. Dried her tears. Rubbed the sadness out of her back. It's the first time their licenses won't be issued by the same state. The first time their cell phones won't be synchronized to the same hour. She doesn't want to live in Mesa. It's too hot. But somewhere north of there, where the desert lifts into the mountains, and the climate starts to take on real seasons. She's talked about this town called Prescott. Without saying anything, she's even sent me links to some real estate listings of houses there, and I've just as quietly deleted them. Sure, I've thought of getting to drive the Speedster much closer to year round than I get to do here, and I'm always pondering life out in the southwest again. But we've still got a daughter here. Another son. A stable of grandkids. The minute we moved to Prescott, she'd be looking East again, sending me 360-degree videos of abandoned houses in Secaucus and factory lofts in Bayonne.

She's given him a brand new Garmin GPS as a going away present. I don't know how many addresses a Garmin holds, but I'll bet a grandkid she's populated as many blanks as possible with the address where we live.

"It's got Blue Tooth," she says.

"Cool," he says, picking up the cue. "I can call you guys from the road."

Here's where my son is one of my heroes. His dad came home from Vietnam with a shrapnel-riddled face and a drug addiction that killed him before he could beat it. Damon was ten. They lived in the solid working-class church-going neighborhoods of Queens that in the early 1980s ended up, like so many, infested with drugs. At twelve, seeing kids his age and younger drawn helplessly to the gold-toothed hucksters who held the street corners, he took matters into his own young hands. He started looking to give kids better things to dream for than gold and shine and bling. He organized baseball, basketball, and handball leagues. He took anything that interested a kid and tried to make it happen. He involved them in block parties. Got them to join his Sunday school. Put together little plays and musicals for them. Directed a youth choir. This may sound all Mary Poppins until you remember where he was doing this — in the drug-ruined neighborhoods out around Kennedy Airport where dealers saw him as a threat because their business depended on making addicts out of the kids he was trying to protect. He knew it. He didn't care. He was fifteen when I came into his life. He finished high school in Mendham, one of Jersey's richer towns, the socio-economic opposite of his old neighborhoods. But he found the same kids there, bored kids, rich this time, kids who got into drugs because there was nothing else to do. This time I got to watch him work. Create a summer basketball league. Raise money for uniforms, equipment, referees. Arrange for courts in local parks and other places. It caught on. Ten teams in all. Kids who didn't want to play kept stats and watched equipment. He got a team from Harlem to come out every Sunday to teach the kids the moves the city teams were using. He had trophies made. He held end-of-summer award ceremonies.

From there he did two years of college and then spent several years in retail management. His start with cars was rocky. He thought oil changes were like smallpox shots — one change made your engine immune for life to future changes. But he learned. He helped build the Speedster. Some of you may remember him from Carlisle — once with his buddy and their Trans Ams and once with his brother. Farmgirls thronged around them on the dance floor at Rod's Road House. They spent two days answering questions about a Speedster they proudly pretended they owned. He was good at anything he did. But if you've done the same thing — as I have — you can tell when your kid is only going through the motions of a life. We knew what made him run. What stood in the way was his mule-headed resistance to parental advice. Then, five years ago, he asked us if we'd help him with one of those "institute" things you see advertised on afternoon tv. It was our opening. Okay. What do you want to do with your life. I don't know. Really. I guess coach. Teach. Help kids. Okay. That's what we'll help you with.

Him, his Accent, the back seat and trunk packed with a computer, clothes, some sports gear, a frying pan and sauce pot, all his lesson plans, a bachelor teacher's essentials. Thirty years ago I came east much the way he's heading west. Solo. The same essentials packed in a rusty old 1961 BMW. A Selectric typewriter instead of a computer. I was about his age. Like him, I was making the move for a dream, a job teaching writing at a SUNY college in upstate New York. For years I maintained the sense that Utah was home. That I'd come east on some kind of visa. That I couldn't let myself take root but had to keep this two-dimensional view of my life here. Then, coming back from a winter visit out to Utah years ago, I got off the plane at Newark. I headed for the door off the second floor side of the terminal that led out to a roof where people could suck down a couple of smokes before heading for the carousels. It was night, the high lights wearing the halos of a cold mist, the whine of the idling jets on the tarmac, baggage trucks trailing their toy carts around me, the deep raw whistling hum of the highways. There it was. That singular response, that forceful sense of a third dimension, that of depth, that of home. Home. I was home. Utah was only where I was from.

If I could collapse thirty years, so that then and now were parallel just for a moment, my son and I might pass each other somewhere in Ohio, a metallic blue Accent and an old green BMW on opposite sides of 80, headed in opposite directions but for the destination of the same dream, not knowing how it will manifest itself. Mesa. You'll make the same mark there you made in Queens and Jersey. Stay long enough, and the west will be your home, and we'll come visit you and build a desert Speedster. Godspeed. We love you.

Land of Make Believe

This is the last opportunity I'll have to address you before you'll have written me in as President of the United States. Yesterday morning, early voting kicked off in Iowa, so for my Iowan friends and supporters who've already voted, it's too late to read this. In fact, by the time this column sees print, early voting will be underway in several other states, and you may have already cast your ballot in my favor. If you have, stop reading, turn the page, keep going, don't look back. What I have to say will only make you check your health insurance plan to see if it entitles you to suicide watch. For the rest of you, those of you who plan on voting, I want you to listen closely.

Don't vote for me.

I'll get to my reasons in a minute.

I was talking to a high school buddy recently when it struck us that nobody from our graduating class had ever run for President of the United States. I rifled through my senior yearbook just to be sure. Not one. Not for lack of potentially good candidates. There were any number of kids who could have stepped up. But Denny Orton chose to become a welder. The Bangerter twins decided to build a rest home empire. Walt Kizerian became a Fred Astaire dance instructor. Dixon Riesnock took over his uncle's rhubarb farm. Hitch Mariano, the kid with the tallest pompadour in the class, became a diesel mechanic. Orval Dastrup decided he'd rather sell Yellow Page ads. Rodney Een did twenty years in the Air Force and then went to work for a golf course. Lavon Wilson became a state trooper. Pud Radcliffe always wanted to sell lumber. It may have crossed Don Wassom's mind to run until he inherited a warehouse full of portable toilets. And the requisite percentage, like any graduating class, chose to become schoolteachers, doctors, criminals, lawyers, postal workers, and hairdressers. Not one of them ever ran for President. Which, of course, left me, and my countdown of reasons you shouldn't vote for me.

21. I love California. I practically grew up in Phoenix.

20. I scrupulously avoid any venue that would call for me to wear something other than Levis and hightop Keds. Wait. We've had that president.

19. I think that gay marriage is something that should be between a man and a woman.

18. Politics gives guys so much power that they tend to behave badly around women.

17. I inhaled. Sometimes I'd forget to exhale. But I always inhaled.

16. I'd raise your taxes to everything you made and give you back whatever you could score on a rolling dartboard with a knitting needle.

15. I'm not worried about the deficit. It's big enough to take care

of itself.

The kids I thought would be naturals for taking a run for President of the United States turned out the most surprising. The Homecoming King has been selling shoes to women since I helped him with his themes so he could graduate. The Student Body President retired with his kidneys gone from forty years of driving a cement truck. The star quarterback went into chicken farming. The yearbook editor became a popular obituaries writer. Mr. Personality repaired jewelry with his fingernails till he went blind. Not that there's anything sad or second-rate about any of their outcomes. But these were guys who, in high school, seemed to already have a foot on the first or second rung of the Run for President ladder. They all ended up stepping down. Which, again, left me.

14. I'm still a fugitive from Grand Theft Cobra.

13. I flunked the psychological screening test to become a Salt Lake City cop back in my twenties because my answers were too psychotic.

12. When people wave at me, I want them to use all their fingers.

11. It is wonderful to be here in the great state of Chicago.

10. I was born in Switzerland to a French mother and a German father and I have the birth certificate to prove it.

9. I have opinions of my own — strong opinions — but I don't always agree with them.

8. China is a big country inhabited by many Chinese.

There were lots of car guys in my graduating class. Larry Hess had his candy apple 40 Ford. Rex Shurtliff had his burgundy 57 Buick. Ben Quigley had his dull black slammed and leaded phantom Hudson. Gary Snook had his chopped 32 Ford with fishscale in its orange paint. Otto Van Ry had his channeled Mercury convertible. Paul Wheelright his little 55 Vette. Roach Jensen his 49 Shoebox. My buddy Bobby his 57 Poncho. Mag wheels hadn't been invented yet so guys ran either moons or spinners on their steel wheels. For the four-spoke spinners, where the spokes were raised so all you had to do was grab two spokes to yank them off and walk away, some of the guys pushed putty into the hollow backs of the spokes and then sank razor blades halfway into the putty. It worked. I always thought a guy like that might run. A guy with a pack of Chesterfields rolled up in his teeshirt sleeve. A guy with a sense of humor. A razor blade president. The kind of guy I'd vote for. Not one of them did. There were all kinds of girls too who were qualified in a cornucopia of ways for a run at the White House. I could get lost in the possibilities of their campaign promises. But it sadly wasn't among the options girls were limited to back then. So here we are again.

7. Babies slug me when I get within range.

6. I didn't realize I was in a Buddhist temple.

5. The companies that advertise in this magazine have contributed to my run on the promise to turn your cars into rolling billboards for their stuff.

4. In my junior year in high school I had to get all my fingers sewed back on.

3. Being president is like being a jackass in a hailstorm.

2. I was never an Eagle Scout.

1. Of all the people I have ever met, you are certainly one of them.

I'd like to think that most of the statements above weren't actually made by guys who ran for — and lived in — the White House. But I can't. Because they were. So this is what I do instead. Close my yearbook, fire up the Speedster an hour ahead of sunset, head west, and lose myself in the foothills that run along the Delaware River, in what I call the Land of Make Believe. The last thing I'd want for company is five black armor plated Yukons. So please. Don't waste your vote. Not on me. Come for a ride instead. That's what we built them for.

2013

Random Acts of God

She was screaming. That was what woke me up. Dressed in black Sansabelt slacks, white shirt, black clip-on bow tie, and a black Eisenhower jacket with a Holiday Inn logo on the chest, the wheel of a Plymouth station wagon in my hands, the first thing I saw was the speedometer. It said fifty something, which should have been okay, except that the front lawn of Litton Industries was in the headlights. She was a Western Airlines stewardess. I was bringing her in from the Salt Lake airport. It was somewhere around midnight. Somewhere off to the left was North Temple, the four-lane highway we'd started out on, the highway from the airport to the Holiday Inn on Redwood Road.

I'd come to work an hour earlier, in the neighborhood of eleven, after cruising State Street with Frank, a guy who also drove what Holiday Inn called an airport limo, sharing a fifth of Old Mr. Boston in my 61 Porsche Super 90 Cabriolet. It was winter. The top was up but the back window was unzipped because Frank was back there, armed with this water cannon of a syringe, firing water at cars as we passed them. I didn't remember getting to work or Barry, the desk clerk from England, telling me there was a pickup at Western Airlines. I remembered driving out of the parking lot, crashing the wagon across some obstacle I didn't know till later was the curbed island in the middle of Redwood Road, pulling up for the left onto North Temple on the wrong side of the left turn lane. That was it. Picking her up? Nothing. The winding access road and then the stretch of highway till the wagon drifted onto the corporate yard of Litton Industries? A blank. In fact, when I heard her screaming, it rattled me, because I didn't know I had a passenger. I got the wagon back on the highway just before it would have plowed through a chainlink fence into a dumpster. Back at the Inn, I stood back while Barry checked her in, and then I asked her if she'd like a lift to where her room was. She looked at me like I was nuts. Barry sent me to the banquet room to sleep it off. At daybreak, sober enough to be making airport runs again, I looked at the wagon. The tires were streaked and caked with mud and grass and yellow paint from the island I'd crashed across.

I don't remember her. Just my lunacy in asking her if she wanted to get back into a vehicle with me. And the way she said no. I've had women tell me no a thousand times since then. Hers is the no I remember. The benchmark no. The ride had also proved to me that God existed. It wasn't the road to Damascus — just the outskirts highway back from the airport — but it did the job. I hadn't disfigured or killed her. She would live to push a drink cart up another aisle. God was real. Starting from the wrong side of that left turn island, His son had taken the wheel all the way to the airport and then back again as far as Litton Industries, where he'd put us safely on the lawn, knowing she'd scream.

We used to bootleg, me and the other limo jocks, because Utah had such a fierce reputation for being dry. Guys flying in to Salt Lake were terrified of even mentioning a drink. But we did it legal. We didn't overcharge. Okay, we were mildly deceptive, but we were only playing it the way they already thought it was. They'd start chatting with you, you'd chat back, and then they'd bring it up. Some would take an academic approach. I understand that Utah has some pretty tough liquor laws. Some didn't beat around the bush. Damn, kid, I'm thirsty. Whaddaya say? Geez, you'd say. I can see what I can do. What do you drink? They'd say what? Yeah, you'd say, in case I get a choice. They'd name Jim Beam or Johnny Walker or Canadian Club. Give me a couple of others, you'd say, in case I can't do that. I'd get them to the Inn and to their room, jump in the Porsche, head for the state liquor store straight up North Temple, buy their first choice, come back, wrinkle the bag up good to make it look like contraband, then knock on their door and hand it over, giving them the price I'd paid for it including tax, rounded off to the lower dollar to avoid a cent of profit and keep it legal. They'd stand there in the doorway to their room amazed and grateful enough to slip you an extra ten or twenty. In your black bow tie and Sansabelts, peddling booze, you didn't dare let yourself feel like God, but what you'd done for a wayfaring stranger a long way from home sure made you feel like one of His errand boys.

You never think of a stewardess as screaming. I lost that Super 90 on a windy Fourth of July afternoon to a sudden sandstorm that rose off the uphill side of Point of the Mountain and came crashing in a blinding cloud of dirt across I-15 where its lanes climbed the flank of the mountainside out by Utah State Penitentiary. My girl and I had the top down. Dirt was everywhere. Blind, mindful of a station wagon I'd just passed, I was slowing gradually to keep it from nailing us when the blue tailgate of a Ford pickup that had panic stopped materialized out of the swirling dirt maybe fifteen feet ahead of us. After the impact I jumped up on the rear deck to wave traffic around us. When the dirt let up I found the girl I'd marry five months later in the footwell. Her ribs were bruised. Her eyes would be black for a while. I saw hair caught in the spider cracks my head had left in the windshield. Little Red Riding Hood was on the radio. The trooper wrote up the accident as an Act of God. The Porsche was twisted too far out of kilter to be saved. I took it apart, sold the pieces off, bought a used Volkswagen that became our wedding car.

When my kid brother Marv started playing with his first band at the Captain's Lounge, the bar at the Holiday Inn, it had been several years since I'd worked there. The singer was a tall black guy with a gone front tooth named Ed who kept fielding requests for Al Green's Let's Stay Together. It was Friday night on a Thanksgiving weekend. My wife and I, there to hear Marv play, sat at the bar. The scattered crowd had some couples but consisted mostly of the kinds of guys I used to fetch from the airport. Later on I would buy and rebuild a rustbucket Speedster and almost kill myself at times. Later still, in another century and what feels like another country, I'd build the Speedster I own now as a way to relive the experience, humbled by the random acts of a screaming stewardess, bootleg runs to the state liquor store, a trick sandstorm, that night at the Captain's Lounge, my young wife next to me, my brother looking proud and cool and scared behind his big new keyboard, this tenuous nexus of customers there for their own reasons, asking Ed to sing Let's Stay Together one more time.

The Tin Man

Classic Auto Upholstery took up some rooms in a hapless cluster of one-story buildings on a back street in the town of Newton. The buildings, all shabby pale yellow with plank siding, were all more or less connected. The street was a shortcut around the heart of town to where Sears and the supermarkets were. I'd driven past the window with the Classic Auto Upholstery sign for several years. Like the rest of the place, it looked abandoned, and I didn't know it wasn't till someone suggested Tommy for doing the interior of my Speedster.

Tommy's a tall lanky guy with a big quick easy grin, and if you can picture Jimmy Stewart with a graying pony tail, you've pretty much got him. It was his place. There was the main shop where all the cars got worked on. Then some smaller rooms that could loosely be called the front office, where photos of some of his prize winning work hung on the walls, the back office, where he did his paperwork, the layout room with a thousand rolls of naugahyde and carpeting and a homemade table the size of a dance floor, and the display room, if only because it had the window where you could read Classic Auto Upholstery from the street. Tommy rented the place from a slumlord. The roof was shot. Sheets of plastic hung half-stapled from the ceiling to keep rain and snowmelt off the cars. Tools, bucket seats, old headliner frames were scattered around. Feng Shui? You bet. Everything aligned in Tommy's head. On one of the shelves on the opposite wall a plastic radio played classic rock. When I got lucky, I'd catch America's Tin Man, like a perfect prize that waited there among the shelves.

The guys who used to gather there for lunch were mixed. Bruce, a town cop, was a sharp looking blond guy who bought old buildings and sang karaoke on the weekends. Tony was portly, on the short side, perpetually upbeat, and sported a baseball cap and a ZZ Top beard with a stripe of gray straight down the center. He owned the detail shop out back and played drums for a cover band called Snake Oil Willie. Todd was this irrepressible lunatic guy who bore a scruffy resemblance to Troy Donahue and got made the butt of a thousand jokes because he was always too quick to take the bait. He drove dumptrucks. Danny was a big balding guy who collected snowmobiles and sold trailers. We'd sit around Tommy's sewing table, a bunch of tacked-together sheets of plywood, and eat pizza or subs or whatever else got agreed on. Tommy sat at his machine while they shared the gift of gab between themselves. Other folks would drop in, like TJ, a tall reserved guy with a permanent tan who owned an excavating company. All of them had bikes. All of their bikes were hogs except for one and that was Tommy's. He had a low-riding stretched-out Vulcan. Me, I had my replica Speedster, right there in that ragtag shop, where it was doing a six-month stretch getting incrementally upholstered.

There were reasons why it took so long. I'd brought it to Tommy raw. He had to drop and level the seat rails. Center the steering shaft. Reglass the eight holes where Donny of Lodi Welding had cut through the fiberglass to weld the roll hoops to the frame. Toni and I had to wade through catalogs of sample patches and wait a month for carpet to come from Germany. Another reason progress was piecework was that Tommy flat out loved the car. Loved having it there in the shop. Loved showing it to friends and customers and suppliers. Sometimes late when things were real he'd say it had a soul. Not soul, like food or music, but an actual soul. Of all the cars he'd ever seen and worked on, it was the only one he ever felt had a living soul.

I joked about how long it was taking him — I even started calling his place the Museum of Classic Auto Upholstery — but I didn't mind him keeping it. It was winter. It was in a warmer place than my garage. And cause never was the reason for the evening. And if you went along with Tommy's thing about soul, then it had soulmates, cars who were there to get worked on too. Mostly they were vintage cars, many stripped, fresh from body and paint shops, others with rusted interiors Tommy had to patch with tin in places. Camaros, Mustangs, some pre-war relics, hot rods, a slammed and tubbed and blown replica of a Willys. Lots of convertibles because Tommy was famous for his tops. But the main reason I didn't mind leaving it there was because it was my ticket. My excuse to show up and hang out. My seat at Tommy's sewing table. I wasn't a biker or a native. I hadn't been born within a 40-mile radius of the shop. My dad hadn't been a county deputy or the owner of a bar called the Toe Hold. I hadn't been around when their stories weren't stories but smoke glass stain bright color things that really happened. When they used the long straight wooded stretch of Hicks Avenue at night as a drag strip and had to send a scout car down before each heat to clear the road of deer and flush out cops. When they made a beer run in a VW bus across the New York border and had to use the beer to extinguish an engine fire on the way home. I had similar stories but they were a couple of thousand miles away. Not that they wouldn't have let me tell them. Not that I didn't want to. I just knew my place. Like my car. Wait and things will always happen.

By the time I got the Speedster back in the spring of 2001 the graft had taken. I was part of them. I started gathering stories along with them — when they were real still and not yet stories. The now legendary propane explosion in the fuel yard next to Tommy's place where the plume drew all the traffic helicopters from Manhattan and the shock wave blew Tommy clean across his shop. The deer that came charging down a wooded hill and broadsided Tony on his bike and put him busted to pieces in the hospital for weeks. Over the years we've done Key West. Duval Street. The Hogs Breath. The Bull. The waitress with the pull-down peasant blouse. The singer who got Bruce to let her write a crack joke on his backside. The butterfly museum on a soapsuds green like bubbles hangover. Tony let his detail business go and runs a Liquor Factory now. He still does Snake Oil Willie. Bruce retired and bought a winter place in Florida he's not so sure he likes. But you can still catch him going down down down down on karaoke. And TJ still spinning round round round round the county digging basements and leach fields. And Todd, still quick as ever to take the bait of an obvious joke, still drives dumptrucks. Danny and the others? Don't know because Tommy's old shop in Newton is abandoned for real this time. Him and his wife got reconciled, pooled their resources and bought a big house north of here in the tropic of Sir Galahad, and he moved his shop out of its Diller Avenue firetrap into his new garage. And after that, there was nothing he didn't, didn't already have.

— Tin Man written by Dewey Bunnell of America

Winter Storm Zimmer

Hunkered down in my igloo of a house, the suicide hot line number set on redial on my phone, I've been wondering ever since that Pennsylvania groundhog lied to us why these winter storms keep coming with the weekly regularity of a snow god on dulcolax. After much introspection I think I know. A wise man told me once to never move through too much stuff too fast without taking time to be forgiven. I think that in my life that's what I've done. Moved through too much stuff too fast. A lot of stuff I haven't stopped or slowed down long enough to ask forgiveness for. I think that's why these storms won't stop. And I think that's why we've got four more to go, not counting Virgil, the one outside right now. Next comes Willy, and then Xavier, and then Yanni, and then the last big one named me. It will be nuclear and apocalyptic, and the brunt of it will hit Pennsylvania on Carlisle weekend, looking to get the biggest bang for its buck when this hobby is at its highest possible concentration. Winter Storm Zimmer is predicted right now to bury the place under all the stuff I've never asked to be forgiven for. Cars, owners, builders, vendors, tourists, children. Nothing will be spared. Not Volvos, not Peugeots, not Saabs, not Fieros.

What I need to do to keep this storm from happening seems simple. Those steps in the twelve step program where you identify everyone and everything you've ever hurt, or dissed, or flipped off, track them down, and ask them to forgive me. The trouble is that my best requests for forgiveness are always rendered on sunny days when it's warm and hazy enough to open the ant bar and start drinking at eight in the morning. Today, one of those straggler days when March just doesn't want to die, thirty degrees and Virgil sowing his oats out there, it isn't the kind of day to make me feel magnanimous about asking to be forgiven. On the contrary. I'm in the mood to do more hurting.

Who do I want to hurt? Easy. The guys who live below and off the sides of that winter cradle the jet stream carves deep into the country. The guys who are out of its reach. The guys who have yet to see Winter Storm Albert or whatever stupid A name they'd give the first Florida snowstorm. You'll see them on the Internet groups we use, the way I'm doing now, watching the YouTube videos they post to entertain the hibernating housebound rest of us. Top down, sunglasses on, out driving in the sunshine, sometimes shirtless, road tunes on the sound track. The coastline of Highway 1. The desert hills of Tucson. Kudzu in fierce bloom along some Mississippi backroad. Miami. That seven mile bridge down in the Keys. What really makes me want to hurt them is when they turn their gopro cameras on themselves to show you how big and hard they can make their grin. Because the date stamp in a corner of the video says January 29 or February 18 or, like today, March 25. Today I could hurt those guys without ever thinking of asking for forgiveness. If I could get to them. But Virgil just carpeted my driveway with a six inch white shag rug, the town's out of plow money because nobody's paid their lake association dues, and Newark Airport's closed. Otherwise look out. I'd resurrect the demolition gang from Bridge on the River Kwai and start with that seven mile bridge. Work my way west. Hit an Alabama gun show for an assault rifle, a sack of grenades, a crate of those IEDs their wives are good at making. From there I'd go after every grin behind every windshield of every topless replicar I could find across America. Here. Hold this pin. Now open wide. I'd track down every YouTube road I could remember and line it with IEDs and gopros so I could put my grin on YouTube too. In California I'd get myself a crowbar and start working away at that San Andreas fault line.

Storms A through V. I don't want to count how many storms that actually comes to in Roman numerals. Here in northern Jersey, of course, we haven't gotten all of them. Some have actually gone south of us. And my buddies in the upper Midwest — the rust belt states of Wisconsin, Michigan, Minnesota, the Dakotas, the New York shoreline of Lake Ontario — have been hit a thousand times harder than we have. By the time most of those storms have made it here to Jersey, they're limping, because they've shot their wads on the streets of Detroit, Minneapolis, Chicago, Rochester. We don't get the serious stuff unless a storm starts circling and evolves into a nor'easter. The guys who do get the serious stuff are the guys who, for some unimaginable reason, choose to live in Wisconsin and Michigan and Minnesota and the Dakotas and Illinois and upstate New York. The American Siberia. What are you guys thinking? Mike? You couldn't have been an architect in Tahiti? Jack? The Dominican Republic doesn't need interior decorators as bad as Milwaukee does? Danny? You couldn't be a cable guy in San Antonio with a year round tan?

Stuff I need to be forgiven for to keep Winter Storm Zimmer from dumping the wintry mix and freezing rain of all my unforgiven stuff on Carlisle. Let's see. Today, if the weather were amenable, I guess I'd start with all the kids I slugged it out with in the parking lots of high schools. We were strangers. In daylight we'd never have recognized each other. It didn't matter. I was there to hurt some nameless kid and get hurt back by him. What were we thinking? I should have taken names so I could track them down and ask to be forgiven. There was the bearded guy I called Jesus one night when Bobby and I were dragging State. Twice, because he didn't understand me the first time, and asked me to call him Jesus again. He had this big mean pickup truck. We had Bobby's Supersport. Until then I'd always thought Jesus forgave and saved sinners. Not this guy. He chased us all over Salt Lake — the Avenues, the State Capitol, the West Side, the East Bench, out to Kearns — before he thought of some other way to waste his time. I could ask Bobby to forgive me, because he's the guy who saved me, but Bobby's already forgiven me for everything. Girls. Little kids. Cats and dogs. Old people. What I did to them is back there, in the mystery in the back of my head, but the weather's too lousy to think of asking anyone for forgiveness.

This time of year we should be pulling the plug on the trickle charger, washing off the winter dust, smacking the fenders to scare out any hibernating copperheads, firing things up, watching the sweeper clean up the road grit. Instead, I'm stuck to the monitor, the windows painted black, the volume up on some hip hop tune while Jimmy cruises Highway 1 in his Speedster, holding a gopro camera on a ten foot pole so I can see the Pacific coast. I marvel at his arm strength. But he's been up and down that highway building up that arm all winter. His lovely wife Ginny rides shotgun. When she smiles at me and waves I wave back. I snarl like a kicked dog when Jimmy shows me his sparkling California grin. Well, if he's gonna be about ten times as smart as a guy who chose to live in Jersey, good for him.

Home from Here

"Your first anniversary isn't your wedding day. It's when you've been married a year."

"This is different."

"No it's not. An anniversary's an anniversary."

Bruce and Lane are continuing a conversation they started online before anyone headed for Carlisle. This weekend marks the tenth time the Speedster Owner's Club has shown up at Carlisle for the event we call Speedsters Meet Spyders. So Bruce is calling it our tenth anniversary. Lane is saying no. He's saying the second time we were here was our first anniversary. The third time second, fourth third, fifth fourth, sixth fifth, seventh sixth, eighth seventh, ninth eighth. This is our tenth time here and our ninth anniversary. But Bruce has this banner hanging across the front of our Carlisle Courtesy Tent. Speedsters Meet Spyders. Tenth anniversary. It's big enough that the Audi guys can see it from their far corner of the field. Bruce is starting to see the light but doesn't like seeing it. Lane keeps turning up the candlepower.

"Like high school reunions," he says, switching it up. "The day you graduate isn't your first reunion. Everyone's gotta go away first for a year."

"But our first time here was our first reunion."

"No. It was the first time we met each other. It didn't start being a reunion till a year later."

Out of patience, Bruce mumbles something, waves his hands like he's batting something only he can see away, and you realize that a conversation there was never a point in starting is finally over.

"See," says Lane, "the cool thing is, we get to use the banner again next year."

"Yeah. Guess that works."

This conversation happened yesterday. I'm remembering it today, on Sunday, as Toni and I head through the Carlisle outskirts on Route 11 toward Interstate 81. I'm in the grip of this awful sadness. A persistent sadness that's been seated deep in my chest since I got up earlier this morning and looked out the hotel window at the Speedsters and Spyders and MGs of my friends under the low congested overcast so relentlessly typical of Carlisle on this weekend in May. A sadness I don't understand and don't know how to mitigate or lose.

I don't know what you call this. When folks start talking about this weekend while the showfield is still snow white, crosshatched with the thin tracks of cross country skis, a field of dreams still a winter and then some away. Or when hotel and banquet accommodations get made before Christmas. Or when caravans that will come from hundreds of miles away, from Fort Lauderdale, Arkansas, Michigan, Rhode Island, the Carolinas, Tennessee, Virginia, and Chicago, start being worked out and scheduled weeks ahead of time.

Or when guys start drooling for Carlisle High School Marching Band egg sandwiches somewhere around Groundhog Day. Or when everyone shows up with something, a gift of some kind, something to give, an offering that can only be had where they call home, moonshine from Tennessee, bourbon from upstate New York, cheeses and microbrews and exotic cigars from God knows where, wines from Vermont. Or when they choose to dip into their talent and create some utterly unique work of Speedster art for the raffle. Or when folks volunteer and collaborate to design custom polo shirts and tee-shirts, mugs, tool packs, grill badges, other souvenirs to commemorate this and every other year at Carlisle. Or when guys are eager to share solutions they've found to automotive challenges, bring parts they've promised each other on the web, jump in when a car's in trouble.

I don't know, like I said, what you call this. At most, not counting drive time, Carlisle is three quick fire days. Everyone knows to value the time together. Nobody wastes it bickering or opinionating. The conversation between Bruce and Lane may possibly have been the closest thing to an argument all weekend. Old friendships barely have time to catch up. New friendships barely get time to forge themselves. Everywhere you turn, there's instantaneous and eager affection, contagious good will, an open smile, a story to hear or tell, this authentic interest in how you're doing, this eager readiness to congregate and bond. Folks whose builds we've been following for months and sometimes years are finally here to show us their cars in person. Saturday night, with its last slugs of New York bourbon, its last big stogies, its last stories, its last flameouts, bleeds deep past midnight into the early hours of Sunday morning. I don't know what you call this. This much exuberance, this much hunger for face-to-face companionship, pent up for a year, looking for release in three days time. My buddy Danny, owner of the meanest Spyder I've ever hurled in, calls us his extended family. Indeed, if we are a family, then I guess what we come together for at Carlisle has become a family reunion. A reunion with its share of oddballs and quirks, old lions and young rebels, but free of crippling dysfunctions and the historic grudges that burn underground for years like peat fields. The best kind of reunion for one reason: the members of this family get to choose themselves. This holds for the Cobra folks, the Valkyrie folks, all the folks brought together under one or another of this hobby's banners.

Toni and I headed out to the field this morning to say goodbye to Jim and Carolyn and the Kit Car Builder crew and, I guess, scavenge what we could off what remained of the weekend. In the raw dank air of the overcast, Kelly and Dave were having their last egg sandwich, Todd and Pineapplehead Jim were hanging out with maybe four lingering Speedsters, and Bruce and Norma were rolling up the tenth anniversary banner. I felt blessed with the best possible weekend. Got to hear Hoss do Geraldine and Moms Mabley. Hear Toni answer with Lucille. Hang with most all my buddies. Make new ones. See Cory and Todd win first place awards for restomod and kit car. I didn't want it over. Leaving, I could see myself out in the showfield, this towheaded gap-toothed kid in worn-out high top shoes, a collarless farmer shirt, short pants hitched up with suspenders, half chasing a departing horse and rider, yelling my young heart out. Nolan! Hoss! Lane! Mike! John! Rich! Carey! Heidi! Tom! Carl! Marty! Lauren! Alan! Mr. Bridges! Lenny! Gordon! Sandy! Jack! Marty! Everybody! Come back!

Now, navigating the insanely unsynchronized stop lights of

Route 11, I'm thinking what Danny said could be the key to this entrenched sadness, this incomprehensible and wild sadness that rides in my chest in a profusion of feelings I don't want to pull apart and analyze too much. But part of it is how brief the time with you was. Part of it is the way you're headed home in all directions, the way you have other lives, the way it feels like you're falling through my fingers and moving out of reach too fast to be recovered. Part of it is worry as you head for homes that are hundreds of miles distant in fragile cars with tiny wipers exposed to ominous forecasts of long black interstate storms. But most of it is what Danny said. Family. Under the familiar Carlisle sky of this heavy gray overcast, heading toward the 81 North onramp, what alleviates this rich deep bewildering sadness more than anything is that you're family, and I miss you, and starting this afternoon and over the next two days, you'll all be checking in to let us know you made it home from here.

Where it Started

Seven to eight years back, in my first column for this magazine, I wrote briefly about the first time I ever saw a Porsche. It happened on an afternoon late in March while I was riding my bike home from eighth grade on the buckled slabs and packed dirt of the sidewalk along a street called Orchard Drive in the Salt Lake outskirts town of Bountiful. The sun was out, warm on my back through my jacket, but my knuckles were cold in air that couldn't hold much heat yet. Passing cars raised dust off the winter grit the sanding trucks had left to collect along the shoulder. My schoolbooks were in a wire basket bracketed to my handlebars, their spines turned forward to keep the wind from blowing back their pages.

It came from behind me. And so I heard it first. The exhaust had this flat repeating bark and the engine this whistling kind of mechanical howl I'd never heard before. I couldn't look over my shoulder because it was a sidewalk you had to continually watch to keep it from bucking you off or yanking you sideways. So I waited till it motored past on the other side of the street.

I've never found the language to describe what happened then. Maybe just the flat-out defiance of something that dared to be that different. This little round car that looked like its roof and fenders and sides and rear had been made out of one continuous smooth unwasted surface of metal and red paint and pulled in snug around the bumpers and rocker panels. Maybe the way it was hunkered down, nothing showy, all business, like all it wanted was to be left alone to do its job of taking someone somewhere. Maybe because on Orchard Drive, a street that was used to Chevrolets, Fords, Plymouths, the station wagons of young churchgoing family neighborhoods, the car looked so out of place it felt sinful to even look at. But in that instant it became the only car I ever wanted. The front wheel of my bike caught an edge of buckled concrete and pulled the handlebars hard left. I had to stop to catch it. I stood there watching until the car went out of sight. And then I couldn't believe I'd let it go. I jumped the curb to the street, stood on the pedals, rocketed off in hot pursuit.

I never caught it. Or saw it again. Orchard Drive ran straight for several miles but the only car I ever wanted was already gone. Maybe it had turned off somewhere. My legs were burning by the time I reached the Safeway on the way home. I searched the lot. I left feeling stupid for thinking that someone with a car like that would ever stop for groceries. I didn't matter. In that one long vanishing glance it had permanently carved its imprint into the soft metal of my young brain. I know that many of us came to this hobby looking to slake the long appetite created by a childhood imprint much like mine. A neighbor with a Cobra. A history teacher with an MG. A high school dude with a hi-boy. An aunt with an Auburn. Some race. Some movie. Or just an anonymous sighting, like mine, where you're left to figure out yourself what kind of car just struck you dumb and stupid.

I never saw the car again. By the time I got to high school, I knew it was called a Porsche, and learned that a red coupe had parked occasionally in the parking lot behind the school. Its owner, a guy I'll call Jeff Rudd, had graduated the spring of that year and was off to college. Unlike me, he'd been a high school hero, varsity football star, leading role in a senior class production of some musical, brooding intellectual, Madri singer, one of those guys who's equally comfortable in shoulder pads and a Key Club blazer, maybe 40 page numbers trailing his name in the yearbook index. There wasn't a record of his Porsche. That was fine. I had my version down cold. For a couple of years, I'd been burnishing the imprint of that single sighting, and I had the car pretty much the way I wanted it. I could even believe it was mine. At night, in bed, I could fall into the dream of driving it, stringing together the European roads that ran through the panoramic photos in the calendars my father got from Switzerland. I admired Jeff Rudd. But I didn't need to know him. Even the little I'd learned about him seemed to make him too real — a guy who could come along, see the dream car I'd lifted like a ghost off his real car, and say okay, buddy, my car needs its soul back. And I needed my dream. From that one galvanizing sighting I moved on to own two actual Porsches — a 61 Super 90 Cabriolet and a 55 Speedster — and build the replica that sits in my garage now.

Years later, in another century, word gets around about the novel I've published, a coming of age story set in the town of Bountiful. I start hearing from people who've read it. People I grew up with. People I didn't know who also grew up around Salt Lake and in the towns of northern Utah. They tell me how they were taken back to their own childhoods. They share their own memories. One of these readers — from out of the blue — is the guy I've called Jeff Rudd. I write him back and for the first time share my story of his Porsche with him. He answers by sending me a scan of an old photograph. And this is where my universe bends. This is where the clock that runs everything reveals its gold and silver wheels and momentarily holds its jeweled movement in place while I try to make sense of time. This is where my dream wraps itself into a Mobius band, where I've followed the path of its surface through three Porsches and several decades, only to end up back where it started, except on the other side. The photograph is the actual Porsche, as it was back then, from the left rear quarter, exactly the way a kid on a bike on the opposite side of the street would see it as it passed him, and it fits the imprint of its memory as if it had been taken with my eighth grade eyes that lucky late March afternoon.

Be All Right

Late last night, unable to sleep, I stole out of bed down to the basement where the engine room for our business is, and without turning the lights on took my computer off standby, fired up Firefox, and caught the onramp onto the Internet. Not sure if I started out northbound or southbound. But I hadn't gone far when Toni was standing next to me, in the dark, a phantom roadside kid in her baggy pajamas in the glow not of headlights but of my monitor.

"Where are you going?"

"Don't know yet."

"Can I come?"

I think I was ripping through Istanbul. I hadn't planned on a passenger. But this was my wife, who can't say no in Turkish, and I couldn't leave her helpless in the rubble on some outskirts road, especially with her sleep hair.

"Sure."

Her smile is quick, bright, happy. She wheels the passenger chair in my office up next to me. We're off. Checking out retirement properties in Ecuador. Watching some street in Damascus get pulverized. Cruising through Victoria's Secret, swimming with dolphins through a sardine school, flying over the Alps so close she gasps. In Paris she wants a bratwurst. Since she's in her pajamas, she asks me to get out for it, but there I am, in my boxers. We find a Wendy's with a drivethrough. We enter the wormhole known as YouTube. Watch a baby elephant try to wake up a dog, Jimmy and Ginny cruise the Pacific coast, and some old dudes formerly known as Procol Harum do A Whiter Shade of Pale.

One of my jobs back when I was in and out of college was moving people for Mayflower Van Lines. I worked for a fly-by-night moving and storage agency on the west side. They had a stable of rundown box trucks and an old Ford semi. Their dollies and hand trucks were beat. Their furniture pads were ragged. Along with Dick and Phil, and Ralph and Larry and Pete, I was one of the lucky regulars. Most of the guys who showed up every morning were day help, either old timers who lived in old hotels in the neighborhood and did their drinking in nearby dives and pool halls, or guys in their early twenties looking for quick cash on their way to somewhere else, or guys in their forties saddled like pack mules with their latest divorces. Most days a line driver with a load from Omaha or Portland or Chicago or Phoenix or some other American city would show up in a big new cabover and trailer that dwarfed our dingy little fleet. For the day help these haulers were the money gigs. Forty bucks cash at the end when the job was loaded or unloaded. When a rig showed up the day help would line up. The driver would look them over and pick what he needed. Usually — based, I guess, on experienced judgment, or on having used them before — he'd pick the old timers. Guys who looked just this side of emaciated, their livers scarred, their faces blasted and their eyes paled from drinking the stuff they could afford. You knew you wouldn't see them till they were broke and thirsty again. Us regulars, with our local gigs, would take the guys who were left.

First stop for the old timers was always the liquor store, for a few minibottles to stop their hands from shaking, their knees from jittering, steady them down enough to move washers and dryers and hope chests. They'd suck a couple of bottles down in the truck. By the time you got to the address they'd be transformed. You'd see their stringy arms, knuckles like rocks from arthritis, hands pumped up with cortisone, stork legs, cobbled backs, and their sudden strength and equilibrium would amaze you. They could strap a refrigerator on their back with a hump strap, head down the flexing walkboard, and go up or down two flights of winding stairs the way you and I might get a glass of water. And stamina. They worked steady as engines and pulled like plow horses all day long. It was what they did. All you had to do was replenish them with a Coors sandwich — five or six beers — at the closest bar for lunch.

My favorite was a guy named Smittie. Straight out of the big band era, Smittie still shaved every day, showed up in creased pants, slicked his black hair straight back in shiny little waves like what lay ahead for the day was a dance hall with women whose evening bags were filled with nickels. In his eyes you could see the twinkle of chandeliers. He could sing every standard I could come up with. He could tell stories that would transport you to Salt Lake's version of Roseland or the Cotton Club with Artie Shaw or the Duke counting down Take the A Train or swinging on Stardust. And then, the break over, without a word, he'd take a hump strap to a television cabinet and be off down the walkboard.

We'll be all right, he liked to say, for no reason, just looking out the windshield, his lips moving with some long remembered song or conversation. We'll be all right.

"Let's go back to bed, honey."

We've come through the wormhole and ended up in the vast showroom of eBay Motors, where I usually end up on nights like this, checking out what Speedster replicas are going for. The last few years this has happened to friends of mine, guys I know in this hobby, the same way it's happened to folks everywhere across the country. When your job goes away, work runs thin a while too long, or your kid can't catch air under the stifling burden that college loans have become, you look for things you can do without. For us, the asset that's usually easiest and quickest to liquidate — and toughest to justify keeping — is that extra car in the garage. You know the one. The one you dreamed and slaved for. The one you were baptized into the Church of the Madness for. The one that will take your heart with it if you cash it in. And that's where I am, torn again, a whiter shade of pale in the light of my monitor.

Toni has taken to playing this game with me lately. She has a set of questions she says will lead anyone to the car that's the perfect car for them. The questions go like this. What's your favorite vegetable. Did you ever own a Hootie and the Blowfish album. Would you ever get a tattoo of a forklift. And so on. She notes down my responses. At the end she consults some application on her crackberry. The answer has always come out Speedster. I've tried tricking it. Giving the wrong responses. It always says Speedster. Everytime I've started to talk defeat — clean it up and sell it — she's brought the game out. Her way of saying keep it. We'll be all right. And that's what brings us home, from eBay Motors, in the Speedster, back to the darkened office, where I remember the guys I used to hump furniture with, where I think of Smittie, where I go through my playlist and pick out Since I Fell for You and ask her if I could have this dance.

2014

November Dusk

The summer I turned twelve my family moved from a sheep and cattle ranch in southern Utah to a new development in an outskirts town north of Salt Lake. We had a dog, a brown long-haired mutt the size of a collie, and my parents thought it would be better to leave him with the sheepherders who'd given him to us as a puppy rather than take him along. He'd inherited a herding instinct from his mother and loved to roam the ranch. My argument — He's my dog! — didn't stand a chance against their logical reasoning. Before we moved I drew a picture of him. I had to keep telling him to sit. He was restless. He didn't understand. He watched me draw, not knowing this was it, not knowing that what I was doing was giving myself a way to remember him. His name was Hank.

"This is perfect," Toni says.

Here in Jersey, down the hill from us, there's a place called Perona Farm. The setting is pastoral, gentrified, with a restaurant that only opens for weddings, fundraisers, and Sunday brunch, and with a reputation for being the best salmon smokers in the country.

Across the road from the restaurant are grass fields bordered with winter trees, an open lot and farm roads paved with oiled gravel, a couple of towering old silos, and a long immaculately white barn. Toni and I have brought the Speedster down. Little jobs I've left neglected have been done. It's been washed, polished, vacuumed, detailed. Thanks to Danny and Lenny the engine starts and runs with more smooth and eager appetite than ever. The description's written. All that's left is the photo shoot. It's afternoon and the November sun is getting low. We look around, at the angle of light and shadow, for the best way to position it. Toni has her iPad. She'll be taking photos because she knows how to use it.

"You know what shots to take?"

"Yeah," she says. "Of the car."

"They say front and back and both sides. And quarter shots from the front and back. And the interior and engine and odometer."

"What are quarter shots?"

"Where you get it from an angle. Like here."

We start with shots of the top up. We want people to see that it's new and tight and clears the two stainless roll bar hoops. Somehow the top gives the Speedster a counterpoint identity, making it rogue, a kind of rascal car, a car that in a cartoon movie would have a tough street Irish accent. We position and shoot it on the open lot. Then coming down the road between the silos. Then with the top off to show the topless lines that have made the Speedster timeless. We do another round of positioning and shooting.

"Let's do the interior and the roll bars. With and without the pads."

"Okay."

We take some shots with the roll bars bare. Then some with the pads in place. Then the full tonneau. The light has started changing. The sun comes almost horizontal and more muted and gold through the bare branches of the winter trees along the edge of the field. We do the trunk, the battery well, the engine, the odometer. Then we stand back. The Speedster sits in shadow. The light that illuminates it now is ambient. The surfaces of the silver curves are liquid with silver tones of pink and gold and white and blue from the colors reflected off the barn and grass and sky and trees and clouds around us.

"Wow," says Toni. "Look. Look how beautiful it is."

"It is."

"Do you think it knows what we're doing?" she says.

"I don't think so."

"Tommy said it had a soul."

"I know."

"He said he's worked on thousands of cars and it's the only one that ever felt like it had a soul."

Tommy Kuka, proprietor of the Museum of Classic Auto Upholstery, the guy who did the interior and trunk. Toni's right. The Speedster has never looked better. The liquid pools of colored light in its polished silver skin gleam with a glow that seems to come from inside it. Like it still embodies the long fierce dream that gave it life.

"I remember."

"Maybe souls can hear. Maybe it knows why we're taking pictures."

I don't often succumb to ascribing human traits to inanimate things. Like giving a car a soul. But this is when I remember Hank. Hank, who herded my brother and me every night to the small room off the back of the house where our bunkbeds were, who watched me draw not knowing the reason I was drawing him was because I had to leave him there. But maybe Toni's right. Maybe the Speedster knows. Maybe it's doing its best to look this beautiful, this irresistibly good, this close to a living thing to make us want to keep it. If so, it doesn't understand, the way Hank didn't, that the decision isn't ours. It's a decision made by forces that are more reasoned and logical than either Toni or I can argue with right now. This car, for me the gateway to an astonishing new world far beyond its silver dimensions, goes up on eBay tomorrow.

Other guys in this hobby have been in this place. Good guys who happened to get caught in the dragnet of this recession, in the losing hand of someone's private equity poker game, on the minus side of some corporate accountant's ledger, without an umbrella in the cold drizzle of trickle-down economics. Guys who love this hobby as much as the next parishioner in the Church of the Madness pew, but sooner or later find themselves in the garage, forced to face the prospect of selling a car whose polished flanks and fenders gleam with the same deep fierce internal glow of a soul in the shadow light from a dirty window. For some of us there might be guilt. For some shame. For others there's the effort to remember back to when we were solvent enough not only to dream but to buy and build what rests in front of us. There's certainly regret. But for all of us there's the expectation that we'll be looking to buy and build again when things get turned around. And that's good. Because selling and buying are the systolic and diastolic heartbeats — there I go again — that keep this hobby going.

Here's my next dream Speedster — if it is a Speedster. It won't emulate the beauty of this one. I don't want to even try to match it.

So the next one will go the other way. Mean and lean and ugly. No upholstery. No paint job except for a couple of rattle cans of red oxide primer every spring and fall. I'll keep the flares. But I'll get the wide five wheels like my original, have them widened out with bands of steel, and paint them to match the rust-colored body. A soul? Yeah. For sure. But I can't think right now of that next one. Not in the presence of this one where it stands glowing in the long shadow of the November dusk.

That Last Story

After more than twelve years, the print run of *Kit Car Builder* magazine ended with the first issue of 2014, when Jim and Carolyn Youngs decided it was time to retire from their long and productive and ultimately undefeated contribution to automotive publishing. "November Dusk," which appears in that final issue, stands as the last "Actual Mileage" story it was my privilege to write six times a year for eight of the magazine's twelve-plus years. I was looking to take the series across the finish line of its eighth anniversary. At forty-seven total, "Actual Mileage" falls one column short of that full eight years.

I wonder what that last story would have been about.

Pimping cars with my buddy Rocky?

Nope. Got that one.

Getting ants drunk?

I'd be repeating myself.

Eating an onion raw?

I'll never make that mistake again.

So I honestly can't say. Coming up with what to write about was always part of the process I initiated two or three days before Jim's deadline. Stumbling down a blank page, leaving a trail of bad ideas, abandoned beginnings, paragraphs that had wandered off cliffs of their own making and lay in rubble below, it took mounting despair in the face of a closing deadline before something would start to clarify itself as "what to write about." It didn't end there. It had to be written. A car had to be worked in. With that process retired along with the magazine, without the worry of leaving Jim with a blank page, I can't begin to predict what that last story would have dealt with. Jim would have to turn the lights back on, do another issue, give me another deadline.

None of this will be happening.

And that leaves forty-seven — one of those "prime" numbers that can't be divided by anything but itself or the number one — as the final count of the "Actual Mileage" run. That forty-eighth story — that eight year anniversary story — will always stay just out of reach along with that next print issue of *Kit Car Builder* magazine. And so this is where I need to say thank you. To Jim and Carolyn. To the folks who read what I wrote and liked it and let me know. Thank you from a teenage kid who, many years before it happened, would read *Motor Trend* and *Road and Track* and *Hot Rod* and fantasize what it must be like to write for a magazine like *Kit Car Builder*.

Acknowledgements

Cory Drake for his cover art. Cory did the drawing as a prize for the Saturday night raffle we always hold at Carlisle. In the days before the raffle he passed it around to collect as many autographs as possible from the Speedster folks. I was lucky enough to draw the winning number for his work. Lucky not only for personal reasons but also because this book could not have a more fitting cover.

The brave men and women who gave me permission to use their full names in this book as they appeared in the stories.

All the other people reckless enough to let me use real or fictional versions of themselves in these stories under their real first names and nicknames.

The New Jersey Replicar Club. The women and men who were its members for the circle of their friendship.

The women and men of the Speedster and Spyder Owners Club for another circle of incredible friends.

The women and men who organized and contributed to the annual gathering of Speedsters and Spyders at Carlisle.

The many clubs around the world that serve as the torch bearers and gathering places for this hobby we call the Madness.

The manufacturers and suppliers who provide us dreamers the means to make our dreams come real.

Jim and Carolyn Youngs for the chance to realize the dream of writing for an incredibly cool automotive magazine.

Readers who liked and were sometimes moved by what I wrote and were good enough to let me know.

Ray Carver and his short story "Are These Actual Miles?" for the heading for my column and the title of this collection.

Danny Piperato and Lenny Cuccureddu for making it possible to bring my kid brother Marv to Carlisle.

Cory Drake again for the author photo on the back cover. The car in the photo is his.

My wife Toni for the rest.

About the Author

Called a raw new voice in American fiction by *Rolling Stone*, Max Zimmer has published stories, poetry, reviews, articles, short biographies, liner notes for jazz albums, and two novels of a trilogy. His first published story "Utah Died for Your Sins" was awarded the Pushcart Prize. He is the author of the groundbreaking trilogy *If Where You're Going Isn't Home*, the ten-year story of a boy growing up Mormon in 50s and 60s Utah with a dream to play jazz trumpet. Born in Switzerland, brought across the Atlantic, raised in Utah, he taught fiction writing at the University of Utah and later, after moving east, at the State University of New York at Oswego. From there, he gravitated toward the city, lived and tended bar in Manhattan, and eventually moved to the northwest corner of New Jersey, where he married his wife Toni and where they now live. His lifetime interest in cars was sparked when he saw his first Porsche from the seat of his bike at the age of thirteen. He went on to own two 356 models — a 61 Super 90 Cabriolet and a 55 Speedster — and build a Speedster replica. Learn more about Max at www.maxzimmer.com.